A GREATER MONSTER

A GREATER MONSTER

Adam Patric Miller

PITTSBURGH

Autumn House Press receives state arts funding support through a grant from the Pennsylvania Council on the Arts, a state agency funded by the Commonwealth of Pennsylvania, and the National Endowment for the Arts, a federal agency.

ISBN: 978-1-932870-92-3

Library of Congress Control Number: 2013950226

All Autumn House books are printed on acid-free paper and meet the international standards of permanent books intended for purchase by libraries.

To my mother

Grateful acknowledgment is made for permission to reprint the following:

"On a Little Street in Singapore." Written by Peter DeRose and Billy Hill. Used by Permission of Shapiro, Bernstein & Co., Inc. All rights reserved. International Copyright Secured.

Parts of this work previously appeared in the following publications: *Agni Magazine, The Florida Review, Pushcart Prize XXXII: Best of the Small Presses, 2008 Edition*, and *Blue Earth Review*.

Excerpt from *Desert Places.* Written by Robert Frost. Copyright 1936. Used by permission of Henry Holt and Company. All rights reserved. International Copyright Secured.

CONTENTS

I have never seen a greater monster or miracle in the world than myself.

Michel de Montaigne

BLESSING THE NEW MOON

On a little street in Singapore,
We'd meet beside a lotus-covered door,
A veil of moonlight on her lonely face,
How pale the hands that held me in embrace.
My sails tonight are filled with perfume of Shalimar,
And temple bells will guide me to the shore.
And then I'll hold her in my arms, and love the way I loved before,
On a little street in Singapore.

"On a Little Street in Singapore"; lyrics by Billy Hill; music by Peter De Rose with Harry James and his Orchestra; Columbia Records, 1939

1

Glenn Gould recorded Bach's *Goldberg Variations* twice: once at the beginning of his career, in 1955, at the age of twenty-two, and then again in 1981, at the age of forty-eight. To coincide with what would have been his seventieth birthday (Gould died at age fifty), both versions have been reissued together—the "alpha and omega" as the critic Tim Page dubs them. In the liner notes to the CD package, one learns that the recording engineers, when they recorded the 1981 version, did not trust the digital technique, which was "in its infancy" at the time. So they simultaneously recorded in analog, a technology at its peak. The new release features the heretofore unheard analog recording for 1981, which, like the 1955 rendition, is digitally remastered. The sound is supposed to be better.

I put on the 1981 recording that I purchased sixteen years ago while in college. Darkly, Gould plays the opening aria, each note placed according to the laws of nature, each note round and full, planetary. But it is not just the piano that sings. A ghostly hum, or at times, a low groan, adds to the ether. The last cadence slows gracefully, the gravity of the moment foreshadowing the true end of the piece when the aria returns, thirty variations later. Just before silence envelops the final note of the aria's first appearance, a beer stein crashes on a table and Variation 1 thumps in: a raucous dance.

2

Wassily Kandinsky, in his introduction to *On the Spiritual in Art*, writes that human souls "are only now beginning to awaken after the long reign of materialism." That nightmare, he adds, "turned the life of the universe into an evil, purposeless game." Our souls are "only a weak light...a tiny point in an enormous circle of blackness." "[W]hen one succeeds in touching them [they] give out a hollow ring, like a beautiful vase discovered cracked in the depths of the earth." Kandinsky published *On the Spiritual in Art* in 1911. That same year, he began to exchange letters with Arnold Schoenberg. Exactly ten years later Schoenberg would be the first to use rows of twelve tones as a method of composition.

3

Gould imbues Variation 15 with sorrow—not the sorrow of regret or nostalgia, but the sorrow of resignation. He reaches, sonically, for something that can no longer be touched. Gould is Orpheus reaching for Eurydice as she is swept back to the land of the dead. Tones repeat. A slow walk, exhausted, shoulders hunched. Tones rise, step by step.

4

In twelve-tone composition, the composer creates what is called a tone row: a series of notes that functions as a kind of musical DNA. The tone row is the original sequence of the piece, which undergoes an almost mathematical reconfiguration and repetition. At the composer's disposal is a range of techniques, including inversion and retrograde. The former flips the musical idea upside down. If a note from the tone row reached heavenward x steps from the last, it now takes x steps down. The latter technique reverses the musical idea, retracing the row's steps from last to first. Schoenberg claims, "[T]he method of composing with twelve tones grew out of a necessity."

5

On my desk at school, I have an M. C. Escher calendar, the type with pages that tear off each day. The artist's name is printed on each upper left-hand corner, followed by the sign for registered trademark: M. C. Escher™. The weekend in my pocket quotes him:

> Hearing [Bach's] music influences my feelings, yet despite or perhaps because of this, the flow of his sounds has an inspiring effect, evoking particular images or flashes of inspiration, and also, more generally,

> stimulating an unquenchable desire for expression...In my periods of weakness and spiritual emptiness and lethargy, I reach out to Bach's music to revive and fire my desire for creativity.

According to the calendar, there will be a new moon on Saturday, the seventh of September, 2002.

6

My grandparents used to live in New London, Connecticut, in an old, three-story house on Ocean Avenue. It was white with green shutters, and a long porch ran along the side of the house that faced the lawn. Just a quick climb over a rusty barbed-wire fence was Dr. Ellison's house, with its pool: a seamless blue into which we would explode in cannonballs.

Each morning my brother and I would wake up in the pink-furnished guest room to the smell of Shalimar perfume cut with nail polish remover. A gentle breeze from the Sound would swell the curtains in toward the beds, into which we had been shoehorned the night before. A vengeance of tucking: if a bomb had been dropped on the house in the middle of the night, we would have been mummified, stiff sheets unmoved beneath our chins. When we woke, our clothes from the day before lay washed and folded on the pink chair.

After our breakfast and her handful of pills, my grandmother would take us to a private beach, where we dug holes and watched them fill with tide, or high-stepped around the sideways scuttle of hermit crabs, or flipped a lone horseshoe crab to watch its writhing legs. On occasion, beyond the sparkling microcosm at our feet, a submarine would pierce the surface on its way back to Groton Naval Base.

After an ecstatic visit to the rides and arcade at Ocean Beach Park (my grandfather breaking the speed limit there and back, gunning his red Triumph) we would huddle in the small room at the far corner of the house, watching TV. Knuckles swollen with arthritis, nails freshly painted, my grandmother would peel grapes and drop them into our cupped hands. They were slippery and sweet.

Later, my brother and I would sneak up behind our grandfather as he sat half-dozing, solving a crossword puzzle, and muss his perfect hair. This angered him to no end. Our grandfather prided himself on his impeccable grooming. He was *dapper*. Eventually, he'd fall asleep, head cradled in the L of his thumb and forefinger. A snore. A grunt.

Sometimes he would rise and walk to his podium, on which rested the behemoth *Webster's New International Dictionary Unabridged*, 1956. Just inside the cover was Noah Webster, expressionless, done up like a founding father. Webster revised his dictionary in 1841, just before his death, noting that it was meant to "illuminate and explain to the American people both their language and their culture."

The dictionary and its podium sit next to me now as I write. I read the definition of "new moon":

> *a* The crescent moon before reaching first quarter; also the phase when in conjunction with the sun. See 1st Moon. *b* Day when the new moon is first seen. Among the Hebrews the period of the new moon was anciently regarded as a religious festival, in postexilic times celebrated chiefly by the women, but still marked by the ceremony of "Blessing the New Moon." The periodical reappearance of the moon is taken as a symbol of the Messianic redemption or renewal of Israel.

Compare that to *Webster's New Universal Unabridged Dictionary*, 1996:

> *1.* the moon either when in conjunction with the sun or soon after, being either invisible or visible only as a slender crescent. *2.* the phase of the moon at this time.

Near the end of his life, my grandfather lost the ability to speak, and then his motor coordination. The last time I saw him, he was propped up in a hospital bed, strapped in. A gown was tied around his neck. I kissed his cheek. It was rough. It smelled sour. My grandmother was spoon-feeding him vanilla ice cream.

It was not long after his death that my grandmother felt her heart fail and decided not to call anyone. Night after night she had prayed for death. She saw no reason to live without him, she'd said. So she lay there and waited. I suppose she must have been annoyed when she woke up in a hospital room. The family came to visit. Then, late at night, everyone gone home, she sat up. She stared (the nurse told me the next day) as though seeing someone. Then she fell back onto the pillow, dead.

At my grandfather's grave in a Jewish cemetery on the outskirts of New London, the Rabbi spoke Hebrew, words vaguely familiar from the bar mitzvahs of childhood friends. My grandmother was angry that day because the Rabbi had insisted on a ceremonial bathing of my grandfather's body.

For herself, she insisted on cremation. No ceremony. No words.

7

A former student of mine went on to study psychobiology in college. One experiment, she told me, examined the brain chemistry of people's reactions to different types of faces. Flash a black man's face at a white woman. Flash an Asian woman's face at a white man.

My student knew I liked Kandinsky, and so she gave me a small book of fine-art stickers that feature his work. I keep them on file in the study. The back of the booklet announces that the stickers are "an eye-catching way to enhance stationery and other flat surfaces." One sticker has been removed from the booklet: an empty rectangle. The remaining stickers are labeled *Subdued Glow, Painting within a Painting, Untitled.*

8

I had yet to buy the reissue of Gould's *Goldbergs.* Like Kandinsky's art as stickers, it would be a repackaging, a sending of the original through a machine.

I used to wear a tie that replicated Van Gogh's *Starry Night.* Another was a Miro. But is it possible to be any further from the smell of oil paint?

The repackaging of Gould's musical epiphanies would, inevitably, include new information about Gould, and about Bach's music. I had read a few things over the years. Bach had composed the variations to help Count Hermann Karl von Keyserling make it through neuralgia-induced insomniac nights in 1742. The music was played by the Count's harpsichordist, Johann Gottlieb Goldberg. The commission came while Bach was visiting Goldberg, his student, in Dresden. Keyserling, in return for the music, sent Bach a goblet filled with *louis d'or.* Glenn Gould liked to soak his arms in scalding water for twenty minutes before he played. He found it relaxing. His arms would be the color of a cooked lobster. And he liked to take pills: pills for his nerves, pills to stop sweating, pills to control his blood circulation. The building where he recorded the 1955 release had originally been a church. Sweaters. Muffler. An electric heater.

9

On the radio this morning, Tim Page was interviewed about his knowledge of Glenn Gould, a brief segment to announce the release of the new three-CD package.

Page only knew him for two years. It was a telephone relationship: late-night conversations of an hour or more, two to three times a week. He finally met Gould in Canada, where the two recorded an "interview" at three in the morning. Gould had scripted the conversation: something like a short radio play. But Page's remarks were based on things he had said to Gould about his work on the *Goldberg* over the phone. So, as Page was at pains to make clear, he was not literally Gould's "mouthpiece" during the interview.

The third CD in the set includes the interview, as well as outtakes from the original 1955 recording session. You hear Gould creating, stopping, and restarting musical phrases. Gould's voice during the Page interview is higher pitched: quick, incisive, clipped—like his playing.

Page says that Gould suffered from high blood pressure and, possibly, Asperger's syndrome, which may have accounted for his heightened sensitivity to the climate.

Gould chose Variation 25 for the sound score to the bombing of Dresden in the film version of Vonnegut's *Slaughterhouse-Five.*

Page characterizes the 1981 version of the *Goldberg* as "autumnal." Gould was a sick man at the time, though most people didn't realize it. He would die of a stroke two months after the release.

About the humming or the singing, Page says that Gould wanted to stop it but couldn't. When you were in the room with him, he says, it seemed much louder.

10

A snow day: the twenty-fifth variation. Months ago I bought a DVD version of *Slaughterhouse-Five.* Books on Schoenberg, Kandinsky, and Gould line my shelf.

11

It was just a few days ago that the second MRI came back. The nurse told my wife over the phone that a small part of our son's brain appears to be swollen. Recently, there has been a change in his tics. Instead of shrugging, or snapping his head forward and back, he crosses his eyes, or they fly to one side as though he is peering around a corner. He says it doesn't bother him. Each night when he practices piano, the tics increase in frequency. Rarely, though, do they get in the way of the music.

Aidan's birth was not easy. After hours of labor, the umbilical cord got caught around his neck, and his heartbeat began to drop. The doctor attached a monitor to the top of his head. They prepared for an emergency C-section. Bach played in the background. When he was born, Aidan smiled, and the nurses rushed him, naked and slippery, to his mother's arms.

I want Aidan to know what I know about music, even what I can't articulate in words. When I was his age, I discovered a recording in my parents' collection of Arthur Grumiaux playing Bach's *Sonatas and Partitas for Violin Alone.* It was a two-record set. The liner notes said that Grumiaux had played a Stradivarius, which accounted for the singular sound. Time and time again, I returned the needle to one particular groove: the fugue from the C major sonata.

When I became good enough to study the first sonata in G minor, my teacher told me that the tension building toward the final cadence of the first movement was like "the cruelty of humanity." He said that his own teacher had told him the same thing.

Bach's *Sonatas and Partitas for Violin Alone* are a violinist's Bible. According to my teacher, they trace the stages of life, from the murky beginning in G minor (the lowest string of the violin is G), though life's climax (the profound Chaconne: the tonalities of the middle strings, D and A), to life's close, the bright E major dances of old age. An optimistic view of the end.

12

> "I am enchanted," writes Kurt Vonnegut,"by the Sermon on the Mount. Being merciful, it seems to me, is the only good idea we have received so far. Perhaps we will get another idea that good by and by—and then we will have two good ideas. What might that second idea be? I don't know. How could I know? I will make a wild guess that it will come from music somehow. I have often wondered what music is and why we love it so. It may be that music is that second good idea's being born."

Vonnegut writes elsewhere that trying to stop war is like trying to stop a glacier. In today's paper, a student protests the war in Iraq by taping her mouth shut. On High Street, people light candles and carry signs. A former student, now a marine, emails from the desert.

13

June 25, 2003. I've played both new versions of Gould's *Goldbergs.* The blue CD (1955) is in the player downstairs, the red one (1981) in the player upstairs. Imagine that they play simultaneously, and that the two flights of stairs are drafted by Escher. Up and down we go: a dragon to a fish to a bird. Black and white modulations; you become me as I become you.

I am at Capital University with Aidan for a week-long music camp. I read through the selected writings of Schoenberg and Kandinsky, while he sits on the floor with the other kids, playing games with the musical alphabet. A parent stalks around with a video camera.

In a letter dated April 24, 1923, Kandinsky writes that he rejects Schoenberg as a Jew. A rift opens between the two. For twelve years, they had been deeply supportive and understanding of each other. It was almost as though a soul of artistic genius had found its twin in the lonely space atop Kandinsky's ever-ascending triangle—"a coworker upon the spiritual pyramid that will one day reach to heaven." But Kandinsky wants Schoenberg to recognize himself as a human being, not a Jew. "We should strive to be 'supermen.' That is the duty of the few." Schoenberg responds, angrily: "[W]hen I walk along the street and each person looks at me to see whether I'm a Jew or a Christian, I can't very well tell each of them that I'm the one that Kandinsky and some others make an exception of, although of course that man Hitler is not of their opinion." Later, in the same letter:

> I am no pacifist; being against war is as pointless as being against death. Both are inevitable, both depend only to the very slightest degree on ourselves, and are among the human race's methods of regeneration that have been invented not by us, but by higher powers. In the same way the shift in the social structure that is now going on isn't to be lodged to the guilty account of any individual. It is written in the stars and is an inevitable process...But what is anti-Semitism to lead to if not to acts of violence?

Near the end, "I shall not understand you; I cannot understand you."

14

August 19, 1912. Schoenberg to Kandinsky:

> We must become conscious that there are puzzles around us. And we must find the courage to look these puzzles in the eye without timidly asking about "the solution." It is important that our creation of such puzzles mirror the puzzles with which we are surrounded, so that our soul may endeavor—not to solve them—but to decipher them. What we gain thereby should not be the solution, but a new method of coding or decoding. The material, worthless in itself, serves in the creation of new puzzles. For the puzzles are an image of the ungraspable. And imperfect, that is, a human image. But if we can only learn from them to consider the ungraspable as possible, we get nearer God, because we no longer demand to understand him. Because we can no longer measure him with our intelligence, criticize him, deny him, because we cannot reduce him to that human inadequacy which is our clarity.

The letter ends with warmest regards.

15

In the 1970s, back when my childhood friend DB prepared for his bar mitzvah (it was to be an orthodox one), I was not allowed to see him. I was cut off. Why? Was it because my mother had converted to Christianity when she married, and therefore I had grown up going to a church and celebrating Christmas? Or was it because my mother had said that Jews expected everyone to feel guilty about the Holocaust, and he had stormed out of our house? Maybe we were separated because his intensive training required it. He was going to become a man.

DB studied cello and he and I, after school, would go over to his house and play duets and listen to the stereo (he introduced me to his passion, Mahler). Or we would burn incense in his bedroom, or talk about girls, or get into his father's collection of pornography.

When his mother died, DB quit playing cello. He moved away. At first, we exchanged notes. Then silence.

16

Somewhere between the third and sixth centuries, the *Sefer Yetzirah (Book of Creation)* surfaced, a short essay that contributes to the tradition of Jewish mysticism. The essay suggests that Creation occurred along thirty-two paths. The author (whose identity is unknown) arrives at the number thirty-two by adding the twenty-two letters of the Hebrew alphabet and the ten *sefirot*—vessels, depicted as circles on the Tree of Life—through which the energy of God flowed in the process of Creation.

For Jewish mystics, each Hebrew letter manifests an internal force, and each letter is assigned a number. *Bet*, the first letter in the Bible, is given the value two. The last letter, *lamed*, has a value of thirty. Again, thirty-two. The interaction of God and the Hebrew language generates Creation.

17

A tiny white pill, one at night before bed, has stopped Aidan's tics. No more jerking around, no more disturbances crossing his face. Looking into his eyes, which are light blue, I see flecks of gold.

18

I listen to Schoenberg's *String Quartet No. 1 in D minor* for the third time, trying to connect with its frenzied meaning. Even though it was written well before Schoenberg's break from the traditions of tonality, the music's complexity offers few clues for ears trained on other centuries. Even Mahler, when presented with the score, said, "I have written complicated music myself in scores up to thirty staves and more; yet here is a score of not more than four staves, and I am unable to read them." Schoenberg's first string quartet was played at a music festival in Dresden in 1906. It caused a scandal.

19

For six years I taught in a public high school in Bridgeport, Connecticut. I drag the cursor over the names of my four students who died, over words describing the violent circumstances of their deaths. The son who was left without a father, the mother who was left without a son. Dreams, images of faces. Now the letters that form their names are gone. Snow gently falls. A

of moonlight buried in the clouds above.

20

For Kabbalists, the number 4 corresponds to Hesed, one of the *sefirot* on the Tree of Life. Hesed represents loving-kindness. We are in a Hesed consciousness when we nurture a child. Hesed must be close to a teacher's heart.

From Hesed, you can travel paths to other *sefirot*: Tiferet (Beauty) 6; Gevurah (Strength) 5; Netzach (Victory) 7. Follow the vertically ascending path from Hesed to the top of the Tree and you enter the realm of Hochma (Wisdom) 2, which forms a triangle, the top of the Tree, with Binah (Understanding) 3 and Keter (Crown) 1. Sometimes the top of the Tree is cloaked behind a veil. It is the hidden part of Creation.

21

Thirty-Two Short Films About Glenn Gould starts with an image of Arctic whiteness. Eddies of wind sweep snow off ice. In the distance, a figure in black (a tiny point at first) slowly walks toward the camera. As it comes into focus, Gould plays the aria from the *Goldberg*.

Slaughterhouse-Five begins with a similar image of whiteness. The camera follows Billy Pilgrim as he trudges through high snow, lost behind German lines during the Battle of the Bulge. Gould plays the ethereal Largo from Bach's *Concerto for Keyboard and Orchestra No. 5 in F Minor.*

The former film conjures Gould's need for isolation, his love of the north, his oneness: Gould comes from a distant white planet and stands, finally, like a solitary black key, a human monolith, an enigma.

The latter shows Pilgrim swaddling himself with a snow-crusted blanket as he wanders in a state of near oblivion. He does not know that he will survive the firebombing of Dresden by taking shelter in a slaughterhouse. Nor is he aware that he will be abducted, put on display, and mated with the "blue movie star" Montana Wildhack on Tralfamadore. Gould plays Bach's Largo again when the Tralfamadorians first appear to Billy as a wobbling ball of light descending from the star-filled night. The ball hovers for a moment, then quickly ascends into the night.

22

My father tried to write about his experiences in World War II, but he couldn't. Last summer, he told me his story:

The impact of it [the bombing of Pearl Harbor] *didn't strike me immediately until I went to the movies...I saw some newsreels—actually, they were probably propaganda films presented as newsreels—of the Japanese throwing up Chinese babies and catching them on bayonets. And immediately I wanted to go take care of that. And I tried to join—I was not yet eighteen. But the moment I became eighteen I enlisted in the Marine Corps. Which was...I don't know if it was catastrophic or remarkably good for me.*

23

The Greeks had a word for the relationship of two men that was extraordinarily close but not sexual in any way...and I can't think of what it is, but that's what we had. I had never to this day, never met anyone with whom I felt the same as I did with Max. But, anyway, well, he was killed on Iwo Jima anyway, so. [Lights cigarette.]

On the ship going over [to Hawaii], *we were standing together at the rail of the ship one night, and we were talking. And he said he liked to sing, and I said I liked to sing. We started singing together. And we found a couple of other guys that liked to sing and we formed a quartet on the boat and continued it when we got to camp.*

His favorite song was "On A Little Street In Singapore." And to this day, I can hear somebody singing that and get tears in my eyes. Our affection for each other, at least mine for him, was that strong—I have no way of knowing how he felt, because he was killed on the first day at Iwo...We took over this house and we mixed up everything we could think of: gin and rum and bourbon and Scotch and Coke and we threw aspirin in—we'd heard if you mixed Coke and aspirin that was supposed to make you drunk in a hurry—that was one of those things you knew in high school. It was untrue, but you knew that. But we spent Christmas Eve [1944] *and well into Christmas morning singing Christmas carols and various other things we'd gotten to harmonizing with, and had just a frightful hangover the next day.*

But it was there that I learned of the efficacy of—oh, what the hell do they call it now, pep pills—dexedrine. We couldn't get dexedrine in any form except inhalers. In those days, I think it was Vicks made an inhaler that was an accordion fold of thin card-

board that had been supersaturated with dexedrine and stuck in there with some kind of flavoring. And this is what you sniffed up your nose. Well, also if you put it in coffee or ate it and drank it with coffee you could get really energized. And I remember one day there was a little guy in our company called Hotoechin. Hotoechin was probably just an inch or two below the minimum size for getting in to the Marine Corps, but he'd gotten in somehow or other. He was a miserable little shit, but he was small and we had this "problem," meaning a maneuver. We had to climb a hill, and I said to the Sergeant, whoever, that I could beat him up the hill. He said, "You lazy sonofabitch, you don't want to go up the hill." And I said, "No, I don't." And he said, "Well you can't make it anyhow." And I said, "Sergeant, tell you what I'll do. I'll make you a bet—I'll put Hotoechin on my back and make it to the top of the hill before you do." I don't know what we bet. I've forgotten. I think I didn't have to do anything but light duty for a week after that if I won. And so I ate two full inhalers of dexedrine. And I was really strung out. I was kicky and ready to go. I put Hotoechin on my back and ran up that hill and I beat him by twenty yards. When you come down off that stuff, it's really terrible. But I didn't have to do anything the next day.

24

About New Year's, we were hot oil, we knew we were going, we were going to ship out...And so we were putting our equipment together and making sure our knives were sharpened, our bayonets were sharpened and our equipment was ready to go and some bags packed up for shipment wherever. And just all in all getting ready to go out and kill people...And then they got us all together and told us we were going to a place called Iwo Jima. We knew nothing about it. We had topographical maps. And we had heard it was going to be a three or four day affair, and we were going to have I think ten or twelve days of bombardment from three or four battleships and two carriers. And they were going to bomb the hell out of the place and nobody would be alive when we got there. Instead of ten days of bombardment, we had three. And the Navy left. The Air Corps continued to drop bombs on the place and strafe it...

We needed the airfields—there were three of them. We were told we'd land on, what was it, Red Beach? Our job was to land and go over the foot of Airfield One and do a blocking move and get this thing over in a hurry.

It didn't quite work out that way...They didn't know that the whole island had been honeycombed with caves, and that they were all dug in, so if we'd had ten, twelve, fifteen days of bombardment it wouldn't have made any difference. Fortunately, we didn't know that.

Early one morning, [we had] *a great meal, the only good meal we had on these ships, steak and eggs, as much as you could eat. Pie. Candy, dessert everything. So in the bowels of this ship it had these amtracks, so called, we hadn't even seen them, tractor propelled. So we circled around for what seemed hours...And at first light, we started in...You never thought of yourself as being one of those who got shot, it was going to happen to somebody else. The only thing I worried about was losing an arm, so, I had just learned to smoke cigarettes and I practiced with paper books of matches, practiced lighting matches with only one hand, both left and right, in case I lost one arm or hand, so I could light my cigarettes regardless to whatever happened.*

When we went in, we went under one of the guns of these battle ships. It was the call of doom. These were sixteen inchers. We were so close we got some of that powder stuff that landed on us that they fired, unburned powder whatever they used to pack the things...About thirty of us, went off the end right into the water, and the treads started going. Some were not properly constructed, or something, and just sunk...[and if you went in] you went down because you were carrying probably a hundred pounds of stuff with you. You had both frag and concussion grenades, you had your ammunition, you had a rifle, your entrenching tool, your pack, your gas mask. Straight to the bottom...I didn't see it happening but heard subsequent rumors around the island, and we had talked to guys who had seen it happen.

As it turned out, we were fortunate in being the first wave, because they waited for more people to come on the beach...until I think about the third wave landed and it was really crowded. Then they opened up with everything. But most of us were not off the beach, because the angle was probably about forty-five degrees and the sand—this is volcanic sand—was in several steps, layers, and you'd climb two steps and slip back three and of course you were scared, and didn't know what was going to happen. Guys lying there, and guys shot, and you'd see dead people and wounded people, and you could hear the cries for MEDIC MEDIC I'M HIT, you know this sort of thing. And the only thing I knew was I had to get off the beach, because that was where they were shooting at us. And we had been told, "Don't freeze on the beach, because you're going to get yourself shot." So we worked our way up the sand and worked our way up the foot of the first airfield...I had at this time lost contact with my whole company. Most people were that way...Later, I met up with my company. We had been fairly well shot up...A few days later we were down to about a hundred ten, and then, when I got hit on the seventeenth day of combat, we were down to fourteen. And most of us were taken out by the white phosphorous mortar shell that blew me off the cliff and got most of the other guys in the company who were left at the same time...

25

On the day that they raised the flag on Iwo Jima we were on what's called corps reserve. We were taken off the line and told to clean up our rifles, sharpen the bayonets and knives and all the crap and relax. And the first night we were there, almost everyone is dug in, I for whatever reason had not dug in, we found a little kind of a pit...But we thought we were in corps reserve, and nobody was going to give us any trouble so we didn't... That was the night they hit the ammunition dump with something and it blew up, so we dug in that night, an hour and a half to dig in—big, deep foxholes. And the second night we were in corps reserve, the Japanese came out of the caves—they had no water, they were dying of thirst. And they would sneak down by ones or by twos, I don't know how many came, and they would try to find somebody they could kill and get their water. And that's when this guy came into my foxhole with me. He wanted my water. That was all. But he came at me with a knife. That's this [points to scar on forearm].

So he struck at me and I blocked it. I was awake, I had just come off my watch. I was lying down. The other guy was looking the other way. I guess he was probably asleep—in corps reserve you don't stand strict watches. But he landed on me, so he stabbed me in the arm. And fortunately the knife stuck there, went between bone. So I did him in. And, actually, first I put out both his eyes, then I strangled him to death.

And it didn't bother me for a while. But within an hour it all hit me. My tongue was quivering, my hands were quivering. I was shaking all over like a dog shitting peach stones. It was only less than a minute, I'm sure. It takes less than a minute to strangle somebody. And I had—my thumbs were all the way through his flesh into his trachea, and so it didn't take probably thirty seconds. And he was screaming, because he was blinded.

26

Rabbi Moshe de Leon of Guadalajara, Spain, claims he did not write the *Sefer Ha Zohar (Book of Splendor)*, which was written around 1280. No, he says it was the book's main character, Rabbi Shimon bar Yochai, who wrote what the Prophet Elijah had revealed to him in a cave in which he had hidden with his son for thirteen years after escaping the Romans. The narrative, as described in *Simple Kabbalah*, "has no linear structure but instead jumps back and forth, delivering information about such topics as the Creation of man, the nature of good and evil, and how our actions affect the destiny of our soul, all couched in stories, expositions, allegories, and little Zenlike koans."

In one of the stories, one Rabbi complains to another that he was annoyed by an "old and simpleton donkey driver" who posed him exasperating riddles, such as, "What commences in union and ends up in separation?" or "What are they who descend when they ascend, and ascend when they descend?" or "Who is the beautiful virgin who has no eyes?" Later, the donkey driver reveals himself to be a learned man. Great insight is to be found within the riddles. The rabbis, upon learning this, fall to the ground weeping.

27

On Saturday, July 19, 2003, at 10:30AM, just above a tree line, I see the moon—just the upper part of a white powder circle in a blue sky, almost transparent.

A few weeks ago it was gibbous. Then, one night: full and bright in a black sky.

Now it performs a slow-motion vanishing act.

28

Disc 3, from the three-CD package, is colored gold and contains two tracks: "Glenn Gould Discusses His Performances of *The Goldberg Variations* with Tim Page, August 22, 1982, Toronto, Canada (50' 47")" and "Studio Outtakes from the 1955 *Goldberg Variations* Recording Session (12' 32")."

On the first track, Page asks Gould what he thinks of his 1955 recording. In an animated voice, Gould responds, "I could not recognize or identify with the spirit of the person who made that recording—it really seemed like some other spirit had been involved."

About this interview Page writes:

> Glenn was dressed in his usual summer wear—two sweaters, a woolen shirt, scarf, gloves, a long black coat and a slouch hat. Moreover, he looked decidedly unwell: his face a mask of bleached parchment, his hair coming out in clumps. Gone was the extraordinary-looking youngster—ethereally beautiful rather than traditionally handsome...In his place was a wise, gentle, stooped man who seemed much older than his forty-nine years, with the air of a delicate visitor ready to cast off his wasted body and metamorphose as pure spirit.

Later on, Gould says rapidly, "The music that really interests me is inevitably music with an explosion of simultaneous ideas—which counterpoint, you know, when it's at its best, is."

On the second track, a click of a control switch sounds into a room with high ceilings, the former church. The recording engineer says, "Goldberg Variation, Aria, Take 1." A twenty-two-year-old Gould plays the complete opening aria. After a rapid Variation 1, Take 1, Gould announces, "I think that's it, but we might try another one." Later, struggling with a variation, he sings it into shape as he plays.

"OK," Gould says. "I think we should've got something between all of those. Now that we have the sort of consummation of this opening section with exactly the same tempo and you have this suddenly militaristic effect, you know—it makes a marvelous climax."

Finally, an exchange punctuated by the sound of the control switch. Gould explains to the engineer that Variation 30 is a quodlibet, a combination of popular songs from Bach's time. The German family, he says, would sit in the living room and harmonize popular tunes together within the same harmonic framework. The tunes for Bach's quodlibet, Gould adds, are "very dirty songs."

29

I have brought four CDs along with me: the red and blue ones from the three-CD package, the disc I bought back in college of Gould's 1981 performance, and the 1955 performance on CD that CBS Records released as part of its *Great Performances* series.

Headphones on, I place the college-bought version in a player, press play, and listen to the aria. Quickly I replace that version with the red CD and listen to the aria. Then I rotate in the blue disk and hear the young Gould's aria followed by the earlier release of the same recording.

Headphones, of course, are not $50,000 speakers. Nor did I use a state-of-the-art CD player. Worse yet, I'm in a restaurant where the sound competes with a country-music vocal, coughing, and conversation. At one table people play cards. A player drums his fingers. At another, a young mother burps her baby. Outside, a woman tilts her head back and blows a vector of smoke toward the yellow canopy.

30

"Did you hit your brother? Huh? Do you want to see what it's like to be picked on by someone bigger than you?" A jolt of pure fear rushes through my body, and before I can react he grabs me hard and picks me up into the air.

At 6'1" and two hundred ten pounds, my father was a physically powerful man. He knew how to leverage strength—I had seen him break a block of concrete with his bare hand. He had taught self-defense classes off and on, and worked the night shift as a security guard. Once, he knocked a man unconscious on the commuter train home from New York. Another time, he gouged the eye of a man who came at him in a parking garage. My father kept an axe handle next to the emergency brake of our car.

He was the one who taught me how to make a fist, how to wrap the thumb tight on the outside of the fingers to avoid a break. And, when I was older, how to hit a man with the heel of the palm to drive the bone of the nose into his brain.

In the mornings, on weekends, I'd snuggle up to him, right in the crook of his left arm, an island rising from the expanse of his body.

He throws me across the bedroom, onto the bed. Somehow, I get around him. I run down the hall to my room and lock the door.

I hear the doorknob turn. Then it stops.

The door explodes as though a bomb has gone off, shards of wood from the shattered frame fly into my room. My father leans against the shattered doorframe and says, "Don't you *ever* lock your door on me again."

31

As though on cue, a long line of a funeral procession—hearse, limousines, cars—takes a left onto High Street past the parked motorcycle cop, lights flashing. Each vehicle flies its tiny purple flag with a white cross. The cop's vest says ESCORT.

I had planned for this section, the thirty-first, to be about Gould's death: about the two strokes; about how, while unconscious, his hand rose and he appeared to conduct; about the first notes of the *Goldberg*'s aria mortised in granite. Both his biography, *Glenn Gould: Life and Variations*, and *Thirty-Two Short Films* use the Voyager spacecraft missions (a recording of Gould playing the C major prelude and fugue from Bach's *Well-Tempered Clavier* is aboard) as a concluding metaphor. Gould's message transcends death as it travels beyond each planet, past the reach of solar winds.

In preparation, I reread the last chapter of the biography. I read about Voyager 1 and its twin, Voyager 2—the first spaceships from Earth sent to explore the distant universe and deliver information about human life. In addition to Gould's Bach and other music, greetings and sounds from Earth were recorded on a twelve-inch gold-plated copper disk. Scientists also sent visual data such as black-and-white images of a circle, a man, a woman with a baby in her uterus, and a twisting double helix of DNA.

In *Slaughterhouse-Five*, the Tralfamadorians live 446,120,000,000,000,000 miles from Earth. Vonnegut's creatures, ("two feet high, and green, and shaped like plumber's friends," each with "a little hand with a green eye in its palm" for a head), would have been good recipients of the Voyager's contents. They would have known what the scientists forgot to include: images of a fire-bombed Dresden, the sound of one man killing another on the island of Iwo Jima.

Billy Pilgrim says that Tralfamadorians think "that when a person dies he only *appears* to die. He is still very much alive in the past, so it is very silly for people to cry at his funeral...when a Tralfamadorian sees a corpse, all he thinks is that the dead person is in bad condition in that particular moment, but that the same person is just fine in plenty of other moments."

This morning, rather than dwell on those particular moments when Gould's condition was bad, I focus on a moment in 1981, when Gould, sitting in the chair that his father made for him, sings with his piano the "dirty songs" of Track 31, the quodlibet. Within Bach's harmonic framework, he transforms the two strands of song into a processional hymn of man's desire.

32

The sky was blue today. Perfect blue, like Dr. Ellison's pool before we would dive in. But now it is dark. Stars dot the sky. The moon set a couple of hours ago. You couldn't see it all day, its lonely face veiled by the absence of reflected light. It is July 29, 2003, and all day the new moon has been and has not been in the clear blue skies.

In ancient times among the Hebrews, preparations for a religious festival would begin with the ceremony of "blessing the new moon." When the slim crescent appeared, it promised Messianic redemption. The sky would swirl and vibrate with starlight and the crescent moon. To celebrate, there was feasting and dancing.

"What?" I can hear the disgust in my grandmother's voice as I consider, momentarily, an ancient Jewish tradition. Once I asked her if she ever went to temple. "I send them a check. That's it. They get my money, not me."

It is late. I pick up the phone and push numbers. A few seconds later, the phone rings in your house. You didn't want to get out of bed. You were exhausted. But maybe it was an emergency. You hobbled around, managed not to stub your toe, grabbed the phone.

"Hello?"

"It's me. Hold on a second. I want to play something for you. You've got to hear this right now. Don't hang up. Hold on."

I walk over to the CD player I bought in college, and put in the red CD. I push the track button thirty-two times, press play, and hold up the phone.

As you stand in the dark, pale hand holding the phone to your ear, I know you'll be patient. I play the entire track, the *aria da capo.* It lasts exactly 3' 45"—a full 1' 35" longer than on the 1955 recording. As Gould plays, I become concerned about the noise in the background: the laptop, the crickets, a car backfiring, a propeller plane, a distant train whistle, sirens. Even the highway on the other side of the river seems loud.

When all that quiets down, finally, Gould's vocalizing. It is as if he were in the room. Some people don't like that. But you keep listening until the end, even though you haven't heard a word from me in years. You listen until that last note is enveloped by the sound of a distant shore.

PROMISED LAND

1

Our librarian, Mary Kowalski, sends a letter to the faculty. Dated August 6, it says she has a request she feels compelled to share. It is her sincere desire to offer no offense, but "simply to be obedient and to find others who feel they are being nudged to serve God through prayer for everyone associated with Fairway High School." During her devotions that morning, she was drawn "to read and reread" a passage from the Bible. Mary quotes the passage in full. It ends: "For he has rescued us from the dominion of darkness and brought us into the kingdom of the Son he loves, in whom we have redemption, the forgiveness of sins." "I believe that we will be greatly rewarded," Mary writes, "when we seek His will for Fairway High School." She says she has asked God to forgive her selfishness and her disobedience. She seeks reconciliation with each faculty member, so she can discern prayer needs for the coming year. She concludes by asking us to question what He would have us do. The answer will be revealed if only those of us who hear His whisper respond by taking a step in faith.

Weeks later more letters arrive. One, from the principal, is printed on school stationery framed by green borders. It asserts: "a quality education provides students with a strong academic foundation, good social skills and the development of assets that will enable them to be happy, productive young men and women." "I am proud," it says, "of the professionalism that the Fairway High School faculty models for our students." It lists opening day events.

Another, from the interim superintendent, says that because of NO CHILD LEFT BEHIND we have new data—data that goes beyond demographics and achievement averages—data that will help us look at the correlation between State standards, curriculum, and achievement. Our efforts to see each student achieve his/her academic potential will be enhanced. It is an exciting time to be in education, writes the interim superintendent, an exciting time to be in Fairway Schools. She looks forward to sharing the celebration of our accomplishments.

2

John and Kathleen next door throw a pre-season party for Ol' Woody, a school bus they have converted to use for tailgating at OSU football games. The bus is painted scarlet and gray. A flag hangs from the side of the windshield. Another flag flies atop a pole in the front yard. I ask John about the yellow flag, and he tells me it's for the place he used to work. He's had a lot of time to prepare Ol' Woody, which has been parked in his driveway for the past week. Now Ol' Woody is stationed on the front lawn. Children climb in and fight to steer the big steering wheel.

Guests wear red. They wear necklaces made out of buckeyes. The driveway is lined with grills for brats and burgers.

Other neighbors, Kevin and Lori, have brought their daughters, Sam and Zoe. Sam, who will start eighth grade, wears a t-shirt that says: HOT PROPERTY. She walks off. Her parents and I talk about the start of school. Sam returns with a paper plate heaped with desserts.

"Sam!" Lori says. Sam smiles.

Lori tells me, after Sam has left, that the two of them spent the day together and it was fine because they did whatever Sam wanted to do, whatever made Sam happy. They got Sam's second piercing for her ears. Lori tells me she got too stressed out when she tried to re-enter the workforce. She has decided to write. Before that, she worked with healing. She says she has a talent for directing the flow of life energies.

3

It is a rainy morning. I drive straight out Brand Road and navigate the roundabout, just completed, adjacent to Wedgewood Village. A video camera points at the road. A sign confirms surveillance. Further up, I pass the "estates" in their varying stages of completion: exposed plywood, a blue tarp draped from an awning, a corporation's logo printed again and again and again on each square yard of its "HomeWrap." A line of saplings promises foliage. A crane loads a rectangular package through a front door.

Opening day ceremony this year is titled "Convention of Excellence." It will take place inside the new high school. A stoplight hangs above the entrance to the school's parking lot wrapped in a bag.

As I walk through the main entrance, I pass the school store: folded shirts, sweatshirts, notebooks, binders—all manufactured with the school insignia. Like a store in a mall an hour before opening, a teacher and helpers check inventory behind a chain-link barrier. Another teacher approaches me to say hello. He asks me how my boys are doing. He tells me about how he and his father would drive through this area years ago. Nothing but cornfields. We join lines of teachers filing into the school's gymnasium.

From my vantage point in the bleachers, I watch male teachers who coach sports hit each other in a play-fight greeting. All the schools are seated together in mock-electoral convention style. We represent states. Teachers wear shirts with school colors: columns of black, off-white, periwinkle, dark pink, kelly green, and navy blue. A netted tube of green, white, and gold balloons hangs above the stage.

The school's marching band plays, and I feel the pounding of the bass drum in my chest. After applause, they march into the aisles, pause in spot with legs pumping, then surge toward the exit. The MC screams the band's name and more applause breaks out.

Signs have been placed throughout the gym: light green paper on a stick with slogans. GO GIRL! WE LOVE DONNA! All of the schools will cast our unanimous votes to nominate Donna, the interim superintendent, as our candidate for the full-time job. Each school sends up two "delegates" to make a short speech. One delegate has a plastic hat with spikes and torch to look like the Statue of Liberty; her partner wears Uncle Sam's hat and coat. Others wear mock-straw hats. Each school's delegates identify their school (one gets a laugh by mentioning that her school is "nestled between four lush golf courses") then praise the school's many accomplishments: last year's crop of National Merit Scholarship Finalists, Commended Scholars, hours of community service. Then all votes are cast, "without hesitation" and "unanimously."

The cinder block walls of the gym have been painted light yellow. Overhead, a maze of ventilation tubes are painted white. The seats are green plastic.

I sit just below the grounds crew: sunburned faces behind full beards or goatees, hunting and fishing caps, tattoos, boots. During the ceremony, reactions range from stoic to bored to incredulous. A young man smirks.

As each speaker approaches the microphone, music from Motown plays over the sound system.

In her speech this year, the union leader chooses a TV show metaphor. She compares "The Apprentice," "Pimp my Ride," "Extreme Make-Over," "Fear Factor," and "Survivor" to what takes place in our school system and what we need to accomplish. "We are in the process," she says, "of an extreme make-over ourselves as we transform these young people." She invites us to join the union.

At the start of the superintendent-elect's speech she jokes about a teacher—"I'm sure many of you know him"—who gave her a Native American arrowhead. "This teacher, as you also may know, is a serious collector of such things, and he would never call such a thing an 'arrowhead'; in fact, as he told me, it is called a 'point.' The punch-line to all this is that he said to me, 'Donna, now when you are superintendent you will always have a point.'" She jokes at her own expense that people always tell her she talks too fast and uses too many big words. "I was, I will admit, pleased to hear someone earlier in today's program use the word 'synergy.'"

She has a vision to shape our school district's destiny as we become a quadrant four organization. It is a six point platform. Each point appears on a screen behind her. She reads aloud, then elaborates. POINT THREE: "Language interactions actually change thought." POINT SIX: "Work is our opportunity to do good in the world."

On the screen the words "DETECTING VIDEO" appear. Photographs of the new school in which we sit, from groundbreaking and ribbon cutting to the erection of walls to finishing touches flash on the screen. It's a high-tech scrapbook: the bordered photographs miniaturize, rotate, cover one another, dissolve. In the accompanying music lyrics refer to a stairway to paradise, a spaceman, the gates of heaven. A final photo of the new faculty and staff in matching shirts centers in the screen and the music changes to "Simply the Best." Then, abruptly, the words POWER OFF? appear, and the people in the photo are called on stage. The music continues. Standing together, they clap in synch as the tube of balloons empties over their heads. As the crowd exits the gym, we hear: POP———POP POP.

4

The summer school people left the thermostats too low, and some of the portables grew mold. Workers came in to scrub the ceilings, to pull out the vents.

The sky turns from gray to blue as I search for the key to my room. On a field nearby a line of students carry bass drums, quickly, backwards. Rhythmic bursts of a whistle. A student's mother, glint of sun off a dome of hair, beige suit, cell phone, spreads out her daughter's schedule for the upcoming year. The daughter: up on toes, crisp clothes, white sneakers, points.

The room is as I left it. Before summer we strip our walls, empty our bookshelves, pack it all in a closet.

I reload the metal bookshelf, hang up student artwork, plug in the CD player.

I dig out student photos. Smiling faces, caps and gowns. Some lie on autumnal lawns, legs in triangles, hands on hips, hands on props.

The PTO serves us lunch. The theme is Hawaiian, so they give us plastic leis. We form a line to the trays of pulled pork and fruit with pineapple. I sit across from Andy Johnson and Kelly Davis. Andy talks about racing motorbikes in Alabama: how he leaned low enough, this summer, to touch his knee. He sent Kelly a picture. Kelly talks about her husband's many bikes. He trained to compete, but had an accident during his first race and broke bones in his hand. Peter Paulson sits to my left. We talk about the new email system, which leads to a discussion of the sub last year who downloaded porn.

On the way back out to the portables, I talk to Cynthia Chen. She's not sure if she should take AP Physics or AP Chem. The latter is taught by Mr. Brennan, who writes romance fiction on the side. He once tried to get me to read a manuscript. I told a student, who was taking Brennan's class at the time, and months later a rumor circulated that Brennan wrote erotica and I was his editor.

At the entrance to the gym I see my former Honors English students, who are on the cross-country team. The girls look thin. Sarah and Erica are wearing shirts that expose their abdomens. When school starts tomorrow, such dress will not be permitted. But now they flaunt it. Sarah's face is washed out. Erica's skin is nut brown. Her left ankle is bulbous from a sprain, "But they said I could run!" she says excitedly. When Erica was a freshman, when she came through my class door she'd yell, "HI MR. MILLER!!!" The girl who arrived at the same time, Krystal Sun, tried to compete with her—so they'd scream in unison. "Who's louder?" As a junior, Erica became more quiet. Tired. People asked her what was wrong. Where was her spunk? As a sophomore she had peaked as a runner; she was the star. Then she slowed.

The girls say they figured out how they are each jealous of one thing about each other. Sarah, no matter what she eats, stays thin. She can even eat a hamburger and go right out and run.

"Hi, Mr. Miller." Emily Smith, another honors student who runs. She's icing her shin. Freshman year she had become involved with Divya's brother Nikhil, but then broke it off because she was Christian and he was not. Nikhil's friends ostracized her. She would stop by after school to talk. She lost enthusiasm for track. Her parents emailed me, concerned that she was losing interest in school. Was that normal?

When I finally make it into my room, I meet Marc. He teaches German I, and he will be in my classroom during my free period. He says he's a workaholic. He not only teaches, but runs a roofing business as well. If he could have things his way, he'd follow his passion and study Latin and ancient Greek. He wants to know if he can use my VCR, and do I have an overhead projector? The French teachers in the middle school are so strict that they've lost six sections of kids for the upcoming year. All that the kids know at the end of the year is that they don't like those teachers. He is an underdog.

Before I head home, I read that we will have a state-mandated fifteen seconds of silence every day during homeroom.

5

In Creative Writing I have students complete a five-minute "automatic writing." Keep the pen moving, no stopping, no self-censoring, go fast. During the set-up I say that going fast helps to overcome the internal censor. I mention late 19th-century France. I tell them that they have been conditioned for years to think in a certain way when they write, that they are too concerned with the teacher and his red pen. They need to access a different part of the brain in order to write something meaningful, something honest.

Mike Keating is in this class, and yesterday we had a meeting about him: every classroom teacher, every administrator, and the coordinator of the Special Needs program. The coordinator provided us with a twenty-page handout that discussed Mike's problem, which is related to his optic nerves. Her reddish-pink lipstick matched her blouse perfectly.

Earlier in the class, when I ask why anyone would want to take Creative Writing, Mike says, "BECAUSE I LIKE TO WRITE!" The words sound drunken. "Oh boy, here we go again," says a student in the back of the room. Her tone is friendly. I say I've got a present for them: colored folders. They each pick a color they like. Decorate them with anything that won't get me fired. "Like what, Mr. Miller?" Sardonic. I know Jason from Honors. "Like don't make lists of people you'd like to blow up." Jason replies deadpan: "I never make lists." Two students, Tim Gaines and Mike Summers, casually blow up balloons. They color them with pens and attach them to their folders.

Later that day, at the end of an honors class, Maria and two friends walk into the room. I haven't seen Maria for two years. I'm happy to see her. She walks up and gives me a hug. The sudden interruption of class coupled with a display of affection makes the new honors students uncomfortable. On a couple of girls' faces, I see an expression of disapproval. Collectively the class seems to say: What's this all about? I dismiss them.

Maria wears a baseball cap backwards. Her face looks drawn. I take her over to where I have her graduation picture tacked up with the others. She looks sickly now, in comparison. The two who are with her stand in the back. One is Don who never talked and still doesn't. He was the silent third wheel who came along with Maria's high school boyfriend. The other, a girl, smiles with bright eyes. She says she was Divya's friend KC. At work, Maria says, a guy asked her to make a sandwich, and she put her head down for just a second, on the counter, took one step back, and collapsed. Out cold for five minutes. At the hospital the nurse missed her vein four times; no blood would come out. It was malnutrition. I look at her. As students trickle in, she asks me how she looks. "I want to talk to you, but not now." "Oh, no.

That means you think I look bad if you don't tell me." "Can you come after school?" She asks Don. Without talking he says they can't. She says she will come back another time.

6

On the way out to the portables, I see Pat Mughan walking in my direction. He looks upset. "Some say the world will end in fire," I say as I pass him. He smiles. When Pat was a freshman, our class went on a field trip to see scenes from the ballet *Romeo and Juliet.* Pat's mother volunteered to chaperone, and became angry when she saw two students holding hands in the cafeteria where we waited for the buses to arrive. "I can't stand that," she said to me. "Look at them!"

Later in the year, Pat will tell me about his visit to the heart specialist who did the procedure on his heart when he was born. Kids with his condition aren't supposed to live past ten. He will have collapsed in the mall, pain shooting up behind his ribcage, writhing on the floor crying. He will not let his mother drag him to the hospital. They'll go to McDonald's instead. While telling the story, he will be wearing flared black pants—skater style. A chain will swing down from a pocket. His girlfriend, Sarah, will not say a word.

Pat will tell me about how he can lower his body temperature through concentrating and how his father angers him to the point where he wants to hit a wall. Sarah stares at me unblinking. Pat baffles doctors with the way his body has adapted to deal with a heart that only pushes blood through his system from the bottom part. He's always warm, which is great, Pat says, because no illness can live there and he never gets sick. Sarah's eyes tear up when Pat talks nonchalantly about death. They will send him to Michigan for a week to monitor him. He wants to be able to recognize anger when it starts so that he doesn't end up having more painful episodes that endanger his life.

In study hall J. R. repeatedly asks Kerry if he can get a ride home. "Can I huh, can I huh, can I?" J. R. is her neighbor and she humors him. Then he's up and out of his seat and talking. I ask him to settle down, give him a book. "I want to draw. Can I draw? Can I draw stick figures? Who has paper? Do you have paper? Kerry, I'm going to draw you." J. R. is a skinny kid who smiles when he sees annoyance rise on another student's face. He's a cartoon. I try to ignore him. He brings me a stick drawing, which he titles "Eight Lil' Guys"—eight stick figures with names like Harry and Elf. Kerry is depicted with devil horns and a pitchfork. I point out to J. R. that one of the characters has arms that form a swastika. "Swastika? What's a swastika? I've never heard of a swastika. What do you mean, swastika?"

"Oh my god, J. R. Don't you know what a swastika is?" asks Kerry.

"No. No. I've never seen one."

"You know, J. R. The sign *Hitler* used. For the Nazis?"

"Oh, the Nazi sign. I know what the Nazi sign is. Of course. Why didn't you just say Nazi sign? The Nazi sign is *cool*."

7

After school Mike Keating's mother stops by for a meeting. She wears a sleeveless, shoulderless shirt that exposes toned arms. Her complexion is pale and flawless, and I can see Mike's face refined in hers. I slide two desks around so that we can sit and face each other.

Mike's mother produces page after page of typed, single-spaced information about her son's condition, all the things that need to be addressed. Last year that aide for Mike was terrible. He never felt like he could ask for anything—she shut him down.

As Mike's mother talks, her eyes periodically tear up.

I try to say a few things to help her understand some of the requirements of the course, but any phrase I say causes her to go off on a prolonged riff about hormone replacement, signs of dehydration, and Mike's inability to decipher idiomatic language.

A student walks into the room. She says, "Oh, excuse me, I didn't know you were in a meeting. I guess you don't have a minute." Before I can say a word, Mike's mother says, with an edge to her tone: "No, he doesn't. We're in a meeting."

"Oh, OK," the student says, with a knowing smile for me—and she lingers for a minute longer, going over to the window to see if her mother has arrived. Mike's mother fidgets impatiently. A pager beeps as the student leaves. "Oh, that's Mike. He's home." She has him page her, so she knows he is safe. Another beeping sound comes at regular intervals from her bag.

She hands me a pamphlet and gives me several pages of lists taken from the internet about Mike's condition. She also gives me a novel in which the protagonist has a similar problem.

Suddenly she has to go to get her younger son who has Asperger's. She stops on the way to the door, several times. She'll email me with more info.

Now she's late; she really has to go. I stand at the door to my room and watch her quick walk change to a jog before she disappears around a corner.

8

Her parents are from Sri Lanka. The dark skin of her forearm full of darker lines of scar tissue. She wears cut shirts and pants, vintage clothing, a phalanx of clothespins. She's in love with a photograph of a British rocker, an anorexic blond-haired boy. A tone of dislocation hovers about the lines of her poems: London, Ceylon, psychoanalysis, needles, and spines. I tell her, jokingly, that I have discovered the secret to her poetry: just throw in a spine. Everything is better with a spine in it. It's automatic. One day she writes her name for me in Tamil: crescent lines, curves and dots. Another day she brings me a map of Sri Lanka she took off the wall of her father's office. I tape it next to my desk and write the words YOU ARE HERE and draw an arrow directed at the Elephant Pass. While I'm teaching, she'll make a loud EEP sound, like the computer does when a mistake is made. Or, as suddenly, she'll scream to her friend across the room, a transplant from Texas, HI, SAM! SAM IS GAY! Her grandfather, she tells me, is also in this country, and spends every waking moment praying. He was a poet in Sri Lanka. Her parents, she adds, have a portrait of Ronald Reagan in the front hall of their house. I tell her it must be boring being surrounded by so many Sri Lankans in our school, that she'd probably prefer more diversity. A rare smile. But when the war subsides enough for her and her family to visit there during the summer, she emails me that she's homesick, has no one to talk to, her boyfriend broke up with her over the phone, and that her chest feels like it is caving in. She had hoped to get some good photographs.

9

On the OSU campus, next to the just renovated football stadium (the playing field lowered, a new shell encasing the old concrete to provide extra seating and exclusive sky boxes) I find a metered parking spot. I feed the machine and lift my briefcase out of the back seat. I grab the coffee off the roof of the car.

I walk uphill, past the gym, past a hotdog stand, to a writing class. Just outside the entrance to Denney Hall, students hang out between classes. They smoke. I maneuver around them into the building, to the third floor, and as I walk the poorly lit hallway, I can see where tiles from the ceiling have been removed: a cross-section of the building up several stories, layers of tubes and bunched wire.

Before class starts, the MFA students talk about teaching their first freshman composition classes. They like teaching; they say it is fun. One has her students bring in a *fact* each class. Together, they go over each *fact*. Each time she says *fact*, it sounds as though she is throwing the word like a dart at a target a few feet from her mouth. She gets excited over the *fact* that a fetus develops "pincers" at the same time that it develops a gag reflex. OR!: did you know the *fact* that a cumulus cloud has a life span? THIRTY MINUTES! When you're looking at it, it is dying. As you're looking at it! Can you believe it? With similar enthusiasm during a discussion of New Journalism, she talks about when she was poor and lacked a topic to write about, when she thought she would eat well and donate blood plasma. That experience could be a good topic. The older woman next to me compliments my briefcase and says it looks like an old-fashioned style, like a briefcase her father used to have.

The professor tells us he is working on an essay about how blind people and disabled people are depicted on TV. On a crime show, a blind person is a murderer.

"Those evil disabled people are everywhere!" We laugh. Then he says he asked his undergraduate class, earlier in the day, Aristotelian questions: what is plot, what is tone? For him, all the categorization is useless.

"I mean what use is it to me to know Fauvism went from 1902–1906 and if you painted in 1907 you were no longer a Fauvist, you were a Modernist?"

When the room quiets down, he talks about the multiple eyes of the narrator. What is writing but diction—the exact choice of words to create tone? He uses the term *fait accompli* and asks if we know what a *tour de force* is. He criticizes George Bush and the Republican Party.

The professor's guide dog, Gustav, rests at his feet. Several times during the class, the dog lets out a comma-shaped whine.

The student who sits next to me (carefully mussed hair, leather coat, torn jeans, portable CD player and headphones) writes articles for the college paper. He said it was cool to interview the rap artist Ludacris over the phone. He said he's mad because in New York you can bring your dog anywhere, but he can't get a smoke anywhere. In Paris, at least you can smoke. He said, "Even though I didn't have time to read the essay, I still think the author's being narcissistic because the essay is basically saying: 'It's all about me and my three-piece suit' and 'Look: look how many times I've been on airplanes and flown first class.'"

At the end of the seminar, the same student inquires about the length of the essays. He is concerned because he doesn't have time to read. What if everyone hands in thirty-page essays? When he asks about a page maximum, the professor gets mock mad. He rises from his seat and says, "I may be blind, but I can still see vague outlines!" He picks up his empty coffee cup and flings it in the student's direction. The cup sails over the student's head, but lightly splatters me and the woman whose father owned a briefcase like mine.

10

In study hall Oona says that she has an obsession with dead bodies, corpses, always has since she was a kid. On Halloween she shows up at school with white make-up on her face and bullet holes (built up on her skin like craters to look real) in her head. I tell her the next day the costume disturbed me because of my students from my old school who were shot dead. That's when she tells me about the obsession, to explain the genesis of the costume. Her hair is highly styled: bangs cover her eyes and in the back it spikes up. She pulls at her bellbottoms, decorated with a hand-sewn pink flare, to show a pink strip on her sneakers. "I match," she says, and laughs. Her clothes imitate those worn by the skater boys, and they de-emphasize the shape of her hips and chest. On the chalkboard she'll write her name with a flourish, and, using a blue pen, draw a cartoon version of herself on a pink post-it and give it to me. Before Thanksgiving break, she'll run up and hug me like we will never see each other again.

11

One afternoon, teachers who coach sports or advise clubs meet in the high school's large lecture room. We are given Tootsie Pops for being punctual and well behaved. We are here to undergo a training—once a year—to better meet the needs of our students. The seats rise up, row after row, and are situated to the stage amphitheater style. A white screen provides a backdrop to the stage.

Teachers lean towards each other, share sarcasm about the yearly *pilgrimage*, or spread work onto their laps. A gray fuzz of exhaustion, fluorescent born, sifts down onto our heads. The speaker is introduced, we are warned about our behavior, the seriousness of what we are about to hear is invoked, and the provider of the treats is thanked.

As the police officer from the Franklin County Narcotics Squad paces and talks, images of colorful pills flash on the screen behind him. Ecstasy. You see, the pills are imprinted with everything from Mickey Mouse to an Acura car symbol to the MTV slogan. Are you with me? And the lingo changes, believe me. Because the drug is "rolled," see, users refer to the high as *rolling*. Get it? *I'm on a wave. I'm enjoying a Tootsie Roll. Let's roll. Let's go roller skating. Let's ride the roller coaster.* Are you with me?

Pictures from a website that sells drug paraphernalia take the place of the colorful pills. Young people party in a club. A few seats to my right, a teacher sleeps.

The officer slips on multicolored gloves with black-and-white zigzag patterns and raised bumps.

Why these? Any ideas? See the eyes on that girl? Completely dilated. Everything's magnified. All the senses. See there on the screen? Are you with me? That guy with the glow sticks is putting on a show for the other guy. And yes, there are freaks. Some kids go just to see the freaks. Are you with me? Look at this fellow—he's shirtless because his temp's elevated, got his Viking helmet with the horns sticking out. And the outfit wouldn't be complete without the mousetraps closed on his nipples, stomach, chest, right? And what's that girl advertising with her schoolgirl outfit and fishnet stockings? That's right. Sex. Are you with me?

The officer is built like a lineman, stout, fifty. He wears jeans. He's got short, brush cut hair, and resembles the actor who used to sell oatmeal on TV. His partner, bald, also stout, more than stout: human bulldog. While the main presenter takes a time out to suck on a water bottle—which now we all know is a sign of dehydration caused by someone on a roll—the human bulldog takes over. His expertise is acid. During one undercover assignment he befriended a kid who was selling and told him a great story about how one night he rode an orange carpet up into the sky, oh yeah, with diamonds shooting right by his head. When he broke the news to the kid's parents, nice respectable people, believe me, never knew, how shocked they were when they toured his bedroom, oh yeah—satanic posters, a wad of money as big as a fist, three thousand dollars, the dresser drawers like a pharmacy. Nice people too.

The main speaker gets to PCP, finally, the drug that scares him. You see, a few years back, when a certain Uncle Donny was watching his two nieces, two little angels, and the mom, you know, just needed a little break, wanted to go out to the movies, and there's Uncle Donny, who's now in charge of the two little angels, there he is shooting PCP down in the living room and he's getting a bad reaction and he starts acting strange and the two little angels come out of their rooms to see what the noise is and when Uncle Donny looks up the stairs he sees two devil monkeys. The girls start screaming thinking a monster must be in their house. "Where is their Uncle Donny?" they think but Donny realizes that these two devil monkeys are there to harm his nieces. So he goes out to the garage and gets a fishin' knife. Well, this story ends up outside across a field where they found Donny just sitting there by a post. I couldn't even look at the pictures, the blood all over the place—my own daughters at that time were about the same age. Donny just come up for parole recently, too. And you can't convince him. He still says there were two devil monkeys that killed his nieces.

Someone hands me a carefully laminated sheet, the paper within saturated with acid and perforated into individual hits. The sheet pictures Alice in Wonderland looking at a mirror. When I flip it over, Alice steps into the mirror.

12

Snow slows the sparse traffic. The surface of High Street is a white gray. Class starts at 7:30. Just inside the door to Yoga On High, there are things to buy: mats, books, videotapes, CDs, clothing. A shirt with a picture of a blue man with an elephant's head.

I hang up my coat. I stow shoes, socks, keys in a wooden cubby. I head down the narrow hallway decorated with photographs of people twisted and serene: a leading yoga instructor—she's an older woman with white hair—sits with legs folded, as do her students. The expression on her face suggests that she could levitate her students if she wanted to, send them right through the ceiling. After a session on another night, I'll see the same instructor on the floor by the coat rack. Several students will watch as she goes in and out of position, rapidly, saying, "Here, then here, then here." Then she will say a word in another language.

My teacher is Mary. A pierced left eyebrow, curly hair, early thirties. She wears what she calls her "muscle shirt" with the picture of the blue man with an elephant's head. Her body is her teaching. She'll put herself into Down Dog position—imagine a dog stretching after a nap with front paws spread forward and its rear end in the air—and say, "What you want to do is let your butt blossom out and back." Her body does as she says. Or she'll curl one arm around another and clasp hands like two flowers curling around each other and say, "It's OK if you can't do this."

At the end of class she'll lower the lights and have us lie flat on mats, blankets folded properly beneath our heads. In measured, musical tones, Mary tells us to let the pelvis relax, feel your butt fall through the floor. Concentrate on your breath. Let your stomach relax. Let go of your butt—don't clench. A loud snoring commences, each week, at this moment. On the first night, Mary tells us to forget about the past, what is going to happen in the future. You've got to allow things to be the way they are if you are going to transcend them.

The floor beneath softens, and I feel my body sink. A cement rage hardens on my chest. I feel a nudge in back of my head. I look down on a body, face down, arms pinned. Snow falls. I hear the sounds of the highway in the distance. I want to leverage the power of my body, but the connection no longer works. I want to push off, strike out. I want to yell. I want to hold on. A wetness gathers on my face until it streams around to the back of my neck.

In the darkness, Mary leans very close to me—her body, her voice, and gently, she reaches under my arms to adjust my shoulders. "Good, Adam," she whispers.

Now I sit on the mat, facing front. The students match Mary's pitches. She says a word in another language, and the others repeat it. The room brightens. We roll our mats and head into the lobby. In the parking lot, I find my car covered in snow.

13

THIS IS THE MURDERING PLACE. In front of the Planned Parenthood clinic a young man, shaggy blond hair, wears a red robe with a gold cross emblazoned on the back. He holds up the sign and talks to a fellow protestor who has propped up a series of bloody photos. Tiny body parts. The light changes, and I continue south on High Street.

When I arrive at the university, the parking lot to the student center is mobbed with minivans, Honda Civics, Accords. A BMW. A Volvo. I park on a side street. Once inside the building I take an elevator to the second floor and walk out into dishes, glasses, silverware clanking and coffee-fueled teacher talk—hundreds huddled around circular tables, each with nametags, French toast, sausage, eggs, fruit. I about-face, push the wrong button and end up a floor above, which provides a view to the breakfast below. I see the gears to a machine, the guts of a clockwork, the teeth of wheels.

Down to the first floor, finally, where the lecture is to take place. The décor is gray and black, a wall of black-and-white photos—the "Professors Hall of Honor"—bloodless, stiff, preserved in liquid nitrogen, forever frozen in the 1950s like the building itself, all brick and industrial gray carpet—it's like turning on a black-and-white TV and finding yourself inside, sitting on one of hundreds of plastic and steel chairs, a white papier-maché wrapped pillar to the right of your knee. The only twenty-first century prop: a laptop connected to a projector that shoots words across a blue screen: REDUCE CONFLICT AND STRENGTHEN RELATIONSHIPS. CONFLICT DOES NOT OCCUR BECAUSE OF LUCK…IT IS INEVITABLE. Then: CONFLICTS OCCUR BECAUSE OF THE EVERYDAY RELATIONSHIPS AND LIFE EXPERIENCES WE CHOOSE TO PARTICIPATE IN OR ALTOGETHER IGNORE. Beneath those messages that disappear only to again and again shoot across the screen is a cartoon cowboy lassoing a cartoon bull, steam out of its nostrils, that tries to run from him.

At one point during the presentation, the speaker says, "We get some interesting verbiage." "Maybe," he suggests, "we didn't pay enough into that person's emotional bank account." He slaps down a list of Irritating Behavior by students that can lead to conflict. "Anytime you interact with people, you get some great stories. That's the beauty part. Now, we're going to look at ourselves."

14

It is nighttime in suburban Bexley. Driveways disappear and houses recede. Road construction. Detour signs. We are lost. I drive out onto a main strip and stop at a gas station. A man with dreadlocks talks to the cashier. An old man, a cab driver, tells me how to find the street. We are a few blocks away.

Alex, a philosophy professor, lives in a less exclusive section of the town, where, as a friend once explained, one could slum it on a professor's salary—live in a split-level ranch in semi-squalor, but have money free to travel wherever you want.

We're forty minutes late. After we walk into the house, Alex's wife Jill, an artist, announces: "Look, we even have a closet, and we can hang your coats in there." Another philosophy professor is there with a man with whom she has been living for eleven years. There are two professors from my wife's department, a couple, soon to be married. They run marathons. Their first early wedding gift to each other is an Aztec, which hunkers down on the shrouded street.

Alex crouches by the fire, while his dog limps around a low table loaded with cheese and crackers. The dog's torn tendon will require surgery. The soon-to-be-married professors have a dog too. Its heart beats too fast. The heart walls are thin. If they let it run, the heart could fail and it could die instantly.

Breathlessly, Jill says, "Oh, why not just let the puppy be happy and run and jump, and if it dies, it dies happy."

"But the condition might be treatable," implores one of the puppy's owners. By coincidence, the best dog heart specialist is right here, right in Columbus—so, with proper medication.

A well-split log on the fire burns efficiently. I wander into the remodeled kitchen where Jill prepares dessert: a chocolate torte, blood orange sauce dripped on top. She caters when she's not making paper for her art. She is slim and has white-blonde hair. A smooth dark stone on a long chain hangs over her heart, and her blouse is unbuttoned to just above her bellybutton. I ask her about her teaching—she just finished an MFA and a friend recently hired her to teach at a local college. Her washed-out blue eyes go wide as she explains that art is the body and language and analysis are in the left brain.

"You know, the Japanese calligraphers talk about the energy radiating down the arm into the brush. Who's to say that that's not just like Pollock feeling the energy drip down onto the canvas?"

Jill then bends low and sways back and forth like Jackson Pollock, acting out the dripping of a masterpiece onto the special aquamarine tile they got for five dollars a square, not fifteen.

"You see, Adam, I've been drinking, and now I'm really on a soap box. I ask my students what do you see? Huh? What do you see? Do you see a frame? Yeah? Well!? What color is the frame? Black? Yes!"

She asks me to pour the decaf into a china decanter decorated with green tigers.

During dessert our host's daughter bustles in and talks rapidly about classes at OSU. An English professor gave her a bling bling quiz on *The Iliad*. You know, who wore what shield, who had a gold bracelet. She got three right, and on the extra credit she guessed that the chest armor that was taken from one warrior was a trick question. The answer was Janet Jackson.

Her parents have put her up in a two-bedroom apartment down the street because they thought it was time she moved out.

The daughter talks about her asshole professors. She says that she tells them to their faces: "I didn't want to come to your class because I didn't want to see your stupid ass face. Kiss my ass," she says.

"What are you on? Did you take speed or something?"

"No, I just haven't slept for days. Maybe an hour a night." She boasts about drinking eight shots of Everclear.

"It tastes just like moonshine."

As she walks across the room, the daughter's shirt hikes up. Her upper body is shaped like a rectangle and a triangle with a small circle on top. It wobbles on two large legs.

My wife talks to Alex about lifting weights to augment his running. He says: "Running is religion." So he invites her up to his bedroom where he has dumbbells. I tag along.

The unmade bed is just under the slanting ceiling as though it were about to be crushed. The bedroom is like a room in a college dorm. Dirty carpet, milk cartons and makeshift shelves for books. A small, unframed landscape with yellows, blues, and greens tacked to a wall. The TV is an old model with two black lines snaking back to a DVD player, a recent acquisition.

He produces two fifteen-pound weights and the training commences. Sitting on the bed, white sheets tossed aside, he hoists the two dumbbells toward the ceiling forming a V.

Later in the evening, the woman from the philosophy department says they have a squirrel problem. Her neighbor shoots them and eats them. Someone mentions an article in *The Atlantic Monthly* about eating squirrel's brains: a delicacy. The final discussion of the evening centers on a group of people who are dying—all of whom need organ transplants. What if they all agreed to draw lots, and for the winners to harvest the loser's organs? Would that be OK?

I open the closet door and reach for our coats.

15

The temperature drops into the thirties. It is the second day of spring. A few flakes blow sideways. Headphones on, I listen to syncopated drum, fast rhythm, singing without words, a synth line—I know what's coming next: a metrical modulation—a whistle stretched, tambourine, piano.

Across High Street: Talita's Mexican Restaurant with the Pepsi logo circle in red, white, and blue. A sine curve of white separates blue and red.

The snow picks up. Flakes flow back up or flow against the breeze. Tall pine trees down Tulane Road sway. Conversation to my right. A woman wearing blue tights warms her feet by the gas fireplace. Coffee grains are loudly banged free like the sound of a gavel demanding order. Behind a partition decorated with pages of non-English speaking countries—words like OBSERVATEUR or CON ESCOBA AL EVEREST or FIN DE SEMANA—there's the table I sat at listening to music and grading papers the night my father died.

I should grade essays. They're in my overstuffed briefcase—sixty-five essays on *Great Expectations*. I need to get grades in. And the paragraphs about poems, self-evaluations, more paragraphs about books.

I concentrate on the music and watch a Dalmatian, one ear flipped pink, weave in and out of people standing in line.

16

THIS IS A LOCKDOWN! THIS IS NOT A DRILL! I REPEAT: THIS IS NOT A DRILL! Students run into class. The lockdown is called while students are moving from one class to the next. I follow procedure. I have to go outside my classroom to lock the door. When I do, I check to the right and to the left to see if any of my students are in sight. I try to stay calm. I lock the door and pull it shut. Inside my students have already begun to take cover—some are sitting with their backs to the wall away from the windows. I flip the light off and turn down the shades. Ryan says, urgently, "Turn off the outside light so they don't know we're here." So I quickly hustle over to the light switch and make sure the outside light switch is down too. My best student, Ben, is over near the window by my desk. "Can we get through this window if we have to?"

"Yes—we can. But we have to stay here and stay quiet for now. There's nothing else we can do."

Outside I hear an adult male scream angrily and at the top of his lungs for students to GET INTO A CLASSROOM NOW! MOVE NOW! THIS IS A LOCKDOWN AND IT IS NOT A DRILL! GO, GO, GO! MOVE!

Ben moves to the back of the classroom and huddles down. I check my computer to see if there is an email. There is none. Standing next to the computer, I feel my proximity to the window, and as I call the main office to see if anyone will answer, I huddle into a safer space. No answer. Then I sit at the foot of my desk.

I check around to see how my students are doing. Only about one third of the class made it in. I hear banging on the door and screaming: "Why won't you let us in!" I hear the girl running away down the wooden ramp outside. My students, as far as I can see in the dark, seem OK. No one is crying. I cross my legs, move the garbage can out of my way, so I can sit with my back against the metal of my desk. I close my eyes and take a few deep breaths. I must appear calm. I think they would only call a lockdown if there were someone with a weapon. I think of calling my wife, but I already hear the sirens. Everyone in the school, students and teachers, has a cell phone, so the word will be out. So we sit in the dark. There is nothing I can do. And if someone comes out and starts shooting?

Twenty silent minutes pass.

Then the principal comes on the PA. There was an intruder, she says. The police were notified. The intruder has been taken into custody. The building is secure and the lockdown is called off. I open my door. My students return. The principal comes on the PA again and says we should return to our normal schedule. Lunchtime will be extended somewhat. We only have five minutes left in class, so I talk to my students and make sure they are OK. Hannah's twin sister Heather comes to the door. She's crying. She wants to call her mother. She thought she'd never see her sister again.

After school, the faculty is debriefed. The intruder entered the building with students coming in from the portables. He was asked to check in and began to act erratically when asked a question about whom he was here to see. He became agitated, combative. The principal says, "When I saw the situation escalating out of control—you know these things are split-second decisions—I called the lockdown. Our school police officer apprehended the intruder, the police were called, and when they arrived, they took him into custody. Apparently, he had no weapons on him. It seemed apparent to everyone at the time that he was under the influence of some substance." Later, I learned the intruder was a black man. He had stripped. He had jumped up and down, saying: I AM GOD and I AM HERE TO TAKE THE CHILDREN TO THE PROMISED LAND.

17

At Michael Foley's graduation party, there is a laptop in the living room flashing pictures from birth to graduation. Three girls, all wearing white, kneel in front of the computer. Michael is a popular boy. He's tall. He looks like the male lead in the most recent Hollywood movie about high school. The top of his left earlobe holds two small silver hoops. He wants to be a politician, he told me in class: a Republican, fiscally conservative, but socially liberal. Watching along with the girls for a minute, I see the names MICHAEL AND TOMMY flash on the screen. Tommy was the friend who died in a boating accident back in middle school. Michael says to the girls, "I know what you're thinking. You wish he was alive." Michael smiles and laughs when he speaks. "That's not funny," one girl responds. "It wasn't meant to be funny," Michael says, still laughing. The picture changes.

In Creative Writing, Michael wrote a haiku titled "Tommy" that had "brain blood" filling a lake. The last line was: "Meghan, stop crying."

In the small dining room there are three heated trays of wings: BBQ, TERIYAKI, and SPICY HOT. A cake, white frosted, spells out CONGRATULATIONS MICHAEL in green words. Out back, below the deck, plastic tables and the freshly cut lawn vibrate with shining sun.

MONSTERS

I remember the first time my father told me he had killed a man with his bare hands. He was tucking me into bed, having brought me Hi-C in a Dixie Cup—the ones that had either a riddle or a joke printed around the base. My room was decorated with monsters, models I had put together with a glue that could have gotten me high. Maybe it did buzz me a little, now that I think back on it, gluing the glow-in-the-dark Werewolf head on. Or maybe it was the black paint for Dracula or the bronze paint for the Mummy. The door to my room featured a six-foot poster of Frankenstein, both arms reaching out, that had been a birthday gift from my father.

"I've got someone I'd like you to meet."

"Wow!"

The excitement over the poster was not the same at night, my door open so I could get plenty of hallway light. I convinced myself that he was there to protect me, the arms were reaching out for any enemy who would try to enter my room while I slept. My brother didn't completely share my monster mania and didn't get into making models. For the sake of safety, though, he did research and knew that by placing rice under the carpet at the threshold of his door (he peeled back the carpet one day for my benefit) any vampire would have to stop and count each piece before he could enter. Rice on the windowsill. Rice under the closet door.

My brother is a chemist for a pharmaceutical company. He works on making or perhaps already has synthesized a drug to reduce pain from chronic arthritis. At least that's what I think it is. It's hard to tell because the information comes second hand from my mother, who got it from his wife, not from Matthew. What did she say to me: "He's a star on the rise"? "It's a huge achievement for him"? One of her permutations. "It's a very big deal"? She says things like that with a hushed, reverent tone, with a touch of pleading for the listener to get the brilliance of her child. "You should call your brother." "Your brother misses you." Another series of lines. Since moving out to Ohio, everyone misses us. "When is your father going to ever see those kids. He's never going to see them again." The hint of death.

Sometimes when I call home, I get my father instead. "Hi, Grandfather," I'll say. When he talks I can hear that his words are wet—I started noticing this a few years ago—a little drool collects in the corners of his mouth. Not a slurring of words, per se, but the words are no longer sharp or clear when they come out. I thought it was an effect of all the painkillers: he wouldn't even notice what was going on with his mouth, like a patient on the way home from the dentist's. "Every once in a while," he tells me, "I forget how many I've taken. My whole body itches." One doctor told him he would no longer write him any more prescriptions. My father told me that he wrote him a very "persuasive" letter. I wonder if he threatened him. He's capable of it—I remember when I discovered a wooden axe handle tucked next to the emergency brake of our Mazda. "This can come in handy," he told me with a smile and then recounted how one late night at the bottom of an off ramp leading into a neighboring city a couple of men had come up to the car in a threatening manner and he had grabbed the axe handle and jumped out of the car. "They left in a hurry."

In the mornings he can't move. When the pills kick in, then he can get about—which now means, when the weather allows, sitting in the yard planting flowers. He's considering having both knees done. Both hips have been replaced. Once he counted out loud the number of times his nose was broken. Football. Martial Arts. He lost all his top teeth to one of the first fiberglass diving boards. But when you take these pills (and I have taken a few myself over the years) there is more than the relief from physical discomfort.

Once my father told me he had been married five times. Once my father told me he had delivered one of his children in his home (this was when he lived in the Philippines) and by the time the ambulance finally arrived the baby had suffered brain damage due to lack of oxygen. Once my father got a phone call saying another one of his children (with whom he had severed all ties—same goes for the wives) had died—the caller hung up—and I remember him circling the house for a long time, dragging on a cigarette, not saying a word. Once, a few years ago—we had been talking about my son while having breakfast at a diner—he said that *that was just like Steven. When Steven was a baby, he would do that.*

In all our time together as a family, some thirty-plus years, he had never once mentioned one of his other children, let alone a name. But it was as though we had been talking about this Steven for years. How many pills had he taken that morning before we got to the restaurant? Several doctors have tried to cut down the painkillers over the years. He told me recently he has three doctors ready to prescribe, each having no knowledge of the other. What is the best metaphor for this? A holy trinity. A three-ring circus. The fates. Hear no evil, speak no evil, see no evil. But things have improved of late, emails my mother from her new computer, "your father has the pain patch. The pain patch is working wonders for him, and he's even reducing the number of Percocet."

"Your father is a pathological liar." My wife said that last night while we were discussing why it might be interesting or difficult to write about his life. "You'd have to do some research." Was he on the battlefield of Iwo Jima, *the bloodiest battle of World War II*? Years ago, standing next to him and two other men chatting about their college days while waiting to tee-off, I heard my father say, without missing a beat, "I'm a Stanford Man myself." Stanford? Didn't he go to war instead of college?

As a child what he told me was gospel, his resonant voice warm, comforting, and as clear as truth. The scar on his arm, a bayonet wound. The man next to him was killed. White phosphorous was removed from his rear-end. "I'm not going to let you look at that one." The man who jumped into his foxhole? "I broke every bone in his body."

He placed my empty juice cup next to Dracula. "I just vant to suck your blood," he said, as he moved in on my neck, tickling me until I screamed, "STOP!STOP!STOP!"

He tucked me in, then kissed me on the lips, cologne strong and sweet lingering in the air. "Sleep tight, don't let the bedbugs bite."

My bedroom dark, he stood for a moment in the yellow hallway light, shielding me from the monster he had glued to my door.

"Open or closed?"

I can see my father now, waiting for the answer from his son, the one who loved monster movies, even though they gave him nightmares that made him call out in the dark.

"Open."

NOT WHAT YOU EXPECTED?

The New York Times this morning: US Air is going under; a scientist accused of mailing anthrax, says he loves his country; a singer gains fame by dying young. A column features writers talking shop. The topic: blurbs.

Imagine being the contestant on the TV show I saw last night. You would stand, illuminated by studio lights, in front of an audience, wearing only black underwear and one sneaker.

Or, re-read the first chapter of that Italo Calvino novel. Notice the way he pulls the curtain back, revealing the author pulling levers, releasing steam, suggesting the dark past, and so forth. On the back, John Updike writes that Calvino "manages to charm and entertain the reader in the teeth of a scheme designed to frustrate all reasonable readerly expectations."

Imagine Updike wearing black underwear as he writes "reasonable readerly expectations."

You should become acquainted with those and with their repercussions. Should the events described above develop and connect in a meaningful, charming way? Are there teeth to this scheme? Who's eating whom? What are you prepared to do about the airline, the scientist, the singer? How will you create the necessary resonance, those essential vibrations, the quality that makes one voice unique among all others? Or are you just going to flail at the keyboard with a Calvino novel splayed on your desk? What did you expect?

You help your child practice the C major scale. It could be D major for all you know, because you were born without perfect pitch. Too bad. You are the type of person deeply moved by the urgency and the darkness of Mozart's Piano Concerto in D Minor, but you cannot comprehend the significance of the key. Sure, minor means sad and you can recognize it when you hear it. But why D? Some composers spell their names with musical pitches. Bach did.

Your spouse returns from work. In the next room pillows are fluffed, a dresser drawer opens, covers are turned down. The wooden bed frame registers the weight of one person.

The contestant works for an airline. I know that you don't. And I know that you didn't fully give yourself over to what I wanted you to imagine. That would be too far out in terms of readerly expectations. The bubble of illusion has burst, for both of us.

DECEMBER FIELDS

Camden, South Carolina, in The Dragon Lady's lair. The air is thick with smoke: Virginia Slims, three packs a day.

The Dragon Lady took care of my father in the end. She brought him to the VA when he woke from an afternoon nap with a fever, his hand hot. Massive pulmonary failure. She kept for me everything she could. The local coroner, intent on seizing all assets, had come knocking. The VA would supply two hundred dollars, a plaque, and a flag. She hid away a watercolor, his last. She saved everything she could in a cardboard box.

Like any good lair, this one was full of hoardings. Paintings in gilded frames, mostly studies of light. The pre-dawn darkness of a shore, black masts just discernible, a woman bent over working, a dab of paint for a cap. A portrait of Saint Anthony as a Franciscan holding the Child Jesus, each with a golden disk for a halo.

Antiques of silver, brass, gold, and pewter. A perfectly lifelike crab fashioned by a Japanese sword maker turned artisan by decree. Two white flamingoes, heads bowed; two white porcelain bunnies, one with an ear stretched out, listening; a centerpiece of white coral, undulating still. Every critter had a Christmas ribbon tied around its neck.

Fukurokuji, the Japanese god of wisdom and longevity, was displayed on a table. His alien-sized cranium was the shape of an egg, carved from dark wood stained black. Downcast ivory eyes, tiny ivory teeth, flowing robes delicately inlaid with mother-of-pearl. He leaned on a staff, holding a persimmon, which The Dragon Lady planned to light with fiber optics.

And there were dragons: carved dragons, a metal-whiskered dragon that spat water into a cast iron bowl, silk dragons that vied for The Pearl of Wisdom, a dragon lamppost beneath a red lampshade. Atop the house was a dragon weather vane encrusted with translucent ruby-colored stones.

From 2AM till 4AM I sifted through the box. Pictures. Letters. Two fishing reels. A kitschy poem ("If you've ever sailed, need I say more/Of your lifeless world when left ashore?") typed on what appeared to be the oldest paper in the box. I read from a journal he had kept when he was living in Amsterdam on a "scholarship" provided by his friend Pat Boone. Years later my father would write Boone looking for funding. Boone responded with a little money to take care of "immediate needs," a "SIMPLE ENGLISH BIBLE," and a letter explaining that God was *the source of all real art. God has everything you need.* Because he was dedicating so much time to God, Boone's cash flow was not what it once had been. That letter, photocopied many times, kept re-surfacing in the box.

This morning the sun conures in the kitchen pierce the air intermittently with their chirping while the TV drones in the living room. One of The Dragon Lady's Pembroke corgis nips the self-inflicted wound on its paw, pink flesh amid thick hair: an homage to my father's absence. I look up from a legal pad, its yellow a match for the petal edge of a yellow iris in the watercolor dated '02.

Tomorrow we meet the probate judge, who will release the ashes. The Dragon Lady will know what to do with them. She knows about many things: Spanish moss, the sandy soil, the history of her converted carriage house, orchids, tapestries, how to show dogs and chickens, how to hunt foxes, how to fire a .38. Last night she produced the silk haori she wears, told me how the fabric was spread out then tied into hundreds of tiny knots, then dyed—the first tie-dyes, really—all pre-WWII, the quality never to be seen again. She shows me one (intricate arching lines) that he liked because of its use of negative space.

The corgis bark, punctuated by the sun conures: bright orange and yellow wedges of sound. Straight ahead, a smooth white lion lets out a silent roar.

After dinner, The Dragon Lady suggests that I eat the chocolate ice cream in the freezer. She doesn't eat the stuff; he did. So I dig around in the freezer, get out the ice cream, open it and see that about one third is gone. I can see where he had scooped. I break into the soft chocolate. I will go back for seconds. The next day I'll empty out the last bits and drop the container in the garbage can.

While I eat, I'm surrounded by corgis. It's part of the ritual: they think I'm him. One gets the bowl, one gets the spoon.

I mailed his last watercolor home, along with a lithograph from 1909 that he had begun to restore: an image of the ocean at night, swell and spume, moonlit. Earlier today at the funeral parlor, the director, brisk and to the point ("Sorry for your loss") had handed me a box about a foot high. He handed it to me carefully, knowing, I suppose, that people underestimate the weight. I balanced it on my right thigh as we rode back to the lair. Tilting it sideways, I read the tag:

CREMATED REMAINS OF: ROBERT E. MILLER
CREMATION # 000108
DATE OF CREMATION: 12/14/2002
1 OF 1

My fingers, perspiring, left marks that slowly evaporated.

In the 1960s my father had studied with Hilaire Hiler. Hiler had kicked him out of his Paris studio. He could not get along with the old artist's wife. Now I take his Hiler Color Harmony Chart over to his window, the one that looks out onto the Camden Polo Field. It is 4:30PM. The sun has begun to set. The color wheel is so old that the numbered colors have faded. *It is only a matter of proportions*, says the chart. *The revolving disk attached to the chart shows how to get the correct color harmonies.* A wheat color predominates, with slim islands of light green.

My flight is delayed, so I sit. I remember the first time I met him, in LAX. I was twenty years old. I spent one day and one night with him. The next day I flew back. Over the next twenty years I saw him a handful of times. Letters. Phone calls. Now, in another airport: brightly lit, glass. White rocking chairs line the wall. I look out at a sky stroked with gray above a distant tree line.

Yesterday The Dragon Lady told me I should take .81 milligrams of baby aspirin every night, religiously. "You've got three boys to take care of. It's good for your heart."

When I asked about the ashes, she said she thought it would not be a good day to sprinkle him around the yard. There was no wind. She will take him up in a friend's Chinese yak of a cargo plane and let the ashes fly from above.

"He'll end up in the treetops—that's where he wanted to be."

I close the book I've been reading and hold it in my lap as the plane accelerates. I correct my posture, straighten my back flat against the seat and face perfectly forward. I relax.

The plane lifts from the runway and, too soon it seems, banks hard to the left, as though the pilot had forgotten something. I look down on the late December fields. Before I can get my bearings, the plane rights itself and sails away.

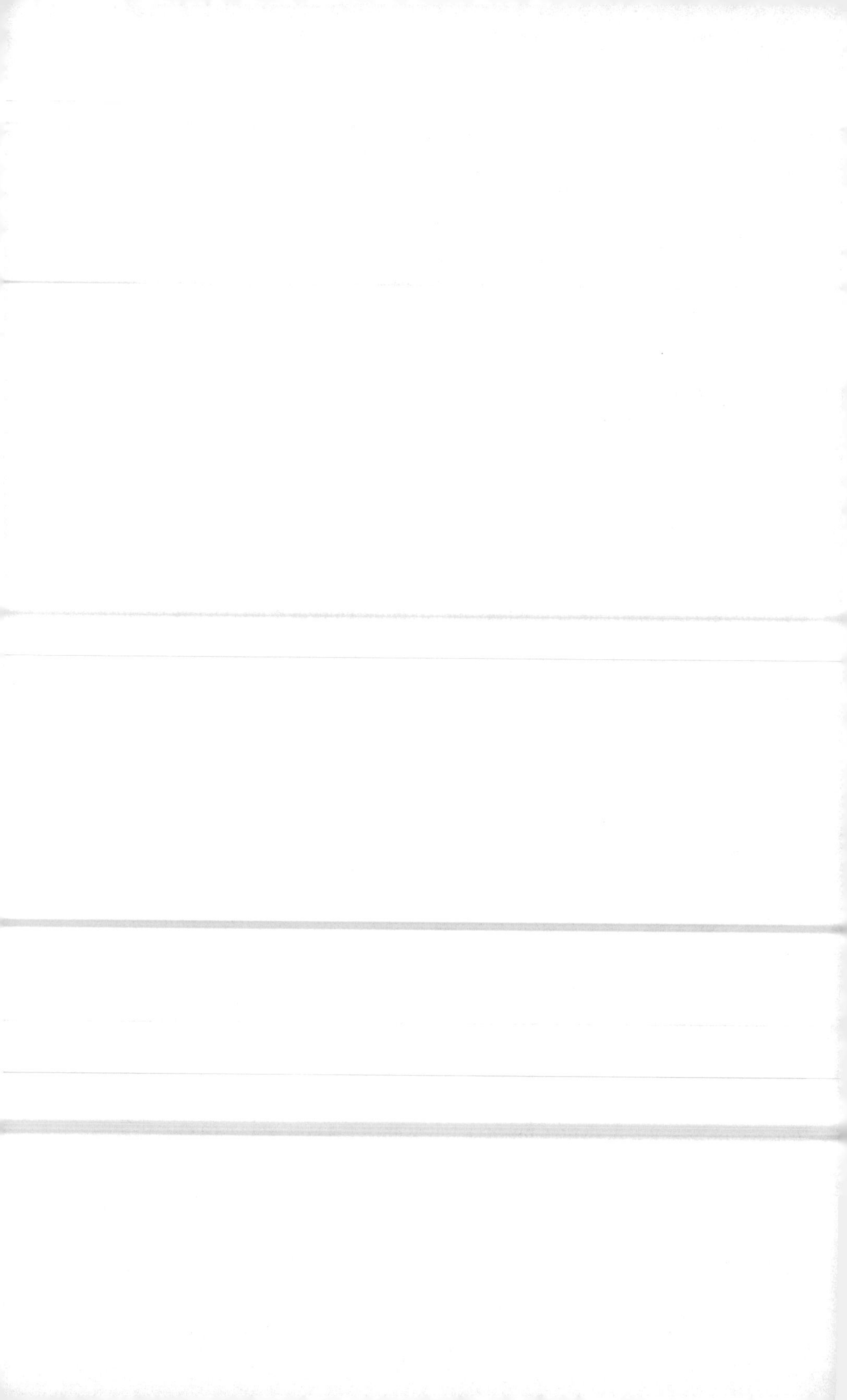

NORTH ON HIGH

A snow day. At least it is for me, not my son. I drop him off and then the day is mine until four. As I watch him run for the doors of his elementary school I see a father I know, and I try to duck him—I don't want to get into it. He sees me anyway and I say with the requisite tinge of guilt, "Yeah, we got off today."

"Wussie."

He knows I teach out in the suburbs, not in the city where our kids go to school. Of course Indianola is not a true "inner city" school. It is an alternative school attended largely by the children of professionals and professors from across the street at OSU. Decent faculty, a top principal, a friendly location (i.e., no real interaction, visual or otherwise, with poverty). This morning the discerning eye picks out a sorority girl slinking back to the dorm, hands clutching her coat shut, head down.

At my son's school, Chess Club is popular. The students are competitive on a national level. Students take private piano lessons. Gifted students are properly identified without delay.

Parents prepare exit strategies for middle school, where all the public schools have been declared in a state of academic emergency. Then it's time to move, or talk to grandparents about money for private school, or swallow a religion class or two.

As I drive north on High Street, trees bend down dense with ice. They almost touch the tops of cars: icy hands waiting to crush down. At breakfast there was an iced encapsulation of magnolia buds outside the kitchen window. The effect of a sudden mass of arctic air in early spring. Crystallization and its weight.

Two years ago, the art teacher at my school committed suicide—he asphyxiated himself in his car. Every day that year, seventh period, I walked by him in the hall (he had hall duty—his job was to check every student's pass), and we exchanged greetings. "Glad you're getting the most out of that college degree," I would say. "Thanks for making our hallways safe for democracy." "How are the cavity searches going?" etc. Most days he had a multi-colored plastic slinky that he unslung across the hall and attached to the other side. No pass, the slinky stayed raised above the ground. He was playful, but he wouldn't let you by. Several times he stopped me. Amusing and childish. He had tremendous arms. Once a student goaded him into flexing. It was "casual Friday" and his sleeves were short, rolled, and ready. When he flexed, he was like Popeye after a case of spinach: one muscle grew on top of another, then another on top of that. "That's not a muscle," I joked, "that's a small metropolis you've grown there." A board member left the news on our answering machine.

The radio plays Haydn's *Cello Concerto in D major.* I pass the Beechwold section of Columbus, with its expensive houses. Attractive, but not yet well hidden at this time of year, a few days past the start of spring. The arctic air has slowed the process whereby this enclave of the upper-middle class manages by late April to disappear from view. Passing by, I'm reminded of back when I taught in Connecticut and I took "Bub" for a ride out of his home city, Bridgeport, into Westport. We drove through Southport and looked at the Gatsby homes overlooking Long Island Sound. As we ascended the curvy road from the beach, we passed Greens Farms Academy, where I had interviewed and been asked if I knew how to sail and if I would chaperone students on a whale watch. Bub and I talked about how one ended up at a school like that, or in those houses. I had wanted to show him things outside the classroom, a different type of education. I remember what my hometown barber told me (he lived in Bridgeport) when I told him where I had landed a job: "You're going to teach in Bridgeport? Adam, those kids are going to teach you."

I can't remember which gang Bub was in: either Foundation or Bush Mob. But I do remember the day three of the opposing gang tried to jump him a few yards down the hall from my classroom. By the time I got there, he had Andre by the throat and was crushing his head against the glass of the door to the music department office. One of the other two Bub had in a headlock, while the third jumped up and down and tried to punch his impervious head. Andre seemed to be in trouble, so I tried to pry Bub's fingers from his throat. I could see blood where Bub's fingernails dug in. The security guard arrived, and he and I pushed Bub down the hall like football players pushing a tackling sled upfield. He finally gave into our requests to let go.

In the principal's office, Bub fumed, his lips caked with white spittle. "So that's how it's gonna be? Three of 'em are gonna try and jump me in the hall? I'ma kill those motherfuckers."

"I'm watching the Oscars," my mother tells me over the phone last night. "Looking at all those beautiful people." That's what it's all about: a look at what's beautiful, a drink of the manufactured fantasy, a drug to relieve us from our imperfect skin, hair, noses, lives. "You could have been one of them." My mother's personal fantasy, born in Hollywood when she got pregnant with me. My father, she says, was being groomed for the movies. My mother a Jewish girl from the East Coast working on the set of *Dr. Doolittle* and *Planet of the Apes.* She dated Tarzan. She saw Charlton Heston breaking stones in his yard. These are the details that she shared with me. Of course I could have been a Hollywood actor: part Moses, part Tarzan, part six-foot-five-inch New Jersey runaway who played the bad guy on "Bonanza." My father had modeled and starred for an extended millisecond in a black-and-white pilot of a Western where he killed Indians, furiously pumping a Winchester for all it was worth (one Spanish-speaking Indian dramatically spreading his arms and slowly, slowly falling dead) until he accidentally found gold in the mountain that he and his F-Troop type companions had to blow up to save their lives. The savages were right on their heels.

I hang up. I turn on the Oscars and see Sydney Poitier deliver the acceptance speech for his lifetime achievement award. The camera pans across the beautiful faces, making sure to hit each famous non-white face it can find. They express awe for this black man, this African-American who achieved so much in an industry devoted to perpetuating images of a white world. I listen to Poitier's words. I see his image on the back of a train, reaching out to help a white man running behind, trying to get aboard.

At the end of the snow day, I arrive home and click on an email from my mother. She wants to make sure that I tune into a TV show called "Boston Public" tonight, because the teacher on the show has students read the book recently published that uses the "N" word as its title. Why does she think I should see it? Maybe she thinks I should be on that show, or at least write for it. Certainly I have plenty of stories. I just told one. But is it true? Is it somehow more meaningful than a TV show? Or is this just like the TV show, repackaging violence for safe digestion, for ratings?

In the suburban school where I currently teach, we prepare for another Columbine with lockdown drills. This is what they call it when we tell our students to sit along the walls of the classroom, no talking, turn off the lights, lock the door. We are not supposed to open the door for anyone, even if one of my students were out in the bathroom when the lockdown drill was called over the PA system. We wait for the administrator to tell us everything is OK.

Of course the students and I recognize the absurdity. I tell them I know what gunfire sounds like, and if we hear shots, we'll have a little race to the woods, which aren't too far from the classroom. "We'll go through this window," I say.

"But that window can't be opened," someone says.

This is true. Our state-of-the-art school is hermetically sealed. The only way to open any window is with a special tool that no one has ever seen. There's supposed to be one at Central Office where (rumor has it) they control the building's climate.

"But," I say, "I've heard if you hit the window with a chair at just the right angle, it will break." A few students concur. They've heard that, too. I realize that what I'm saying could get me into trouble. One simply does not question administrative wisdom.

When I was new to the school, I went to an administrator and suggested that it would be easy for someone to drop chemicals in the ventilation system. My thinking lacked decorum.

Everything is fine. If we maintain our surface calm, Columbine remains a TV event. Parental fears are quashed by lockdown drills. Images of students in the "inner city" are disseminated through "Boston Public."

Before I drove my son to school this morning, I ran out and started the car so it could warm up. It was covered with a coat of ice. Aidan was cold while he ate his cereal and asked me to get him a sweater. He said this out loud. I was glad he was talking. When he first got up, he wouldn't say anything to me. He sat up in bed after some prodding. I kissed him. I tried to tickle him. No words. In the kitchen, I asked him what cereal he'd like. He walked away without a word. He returned with a pencil, and, on the front page of the *The New York Times*, wrote in his seven-year-old hand: LIFE.

As we drove to school, he said nothing. I was remembering Richard T. from Bridgeport, with his hoodie and his headphones. The day he arrived (like so many others transferring in and out of class all year long) I asked him to take off his hat. He ignored me. I told him if he didn't want to take his hat off or put his Walkman away that he'd have to explain his thinking to the administrator. Off he went.

When Richard returned, he announced to me and to the class that if I ever got him in trouble again, he'd blow me up. And when he got out of prison, he'd find my family and blow them up too. It was quiet for a second until one student, Amelia, said "Richard, that ain't right. You don't say that to a teacher."

"Richard, come out into the hall with me for a second." He followed me out into the hall and I closed the door. He leaned against a locker and slouched down a bit. "Richard, I've got to know if you're being serious. Are you threatening me and my family? I've got to know the truth—because if you are serious, we've got a problem. You know, a teacher is supposed to help students. That's my job. And then you're going to threaten me like that in front of the whole class? We barely even know each other."

"Nah, nah. I was just joking with you."

He glanced up at me almost from a crouch as though preparing an uppercut. It was a sly look, a practiced look, a faint smile on his face. His eyes unnerved me. A threat flashed in them.

For a brief moment, the suddenness of which stunned me, I thought I would reach for his throat right then and there and strangle him with the intensity that Bub brought to bear on Andre.

"Come on. Let's go back inside."

Another day, Richard mimicked everything I did. He became my mirror image. When I spoke, his lips moved as if he were saying what I was saying. When I motioned with my hands, he made the same motion. It was like an experiment that actors in training would do.

I noticed and played along, trying to make light of it. The other students were our audience. I moved in odd ways, and Richard matched me, move for move. Then he added audio. Richard was me and, as it turned out, I was ridiculous. The audience began to laugh.

I started to ask around about Richard. A social worker broke a confidentiality agreement to warn me. In all the years he had worked with young people, he said only Richard had scared him. He talked constantly about committing crimes, about how he loved the power he felt when he held a gun to someone. He said he'd be dead before he was twenty-one and didn't care if he took someone with him. His girlfriend's baby was born dead, and he had laughed about it.

I found out that the time I sent Richard out of my class, his parole officer had been checking with the administrator on his progress. He had been given only one chance at our school, and with that incident documented, he would be expelled. I was the cause. The principal told me that security would do its best to keep Richard off school grounds, but there weren't guarantees.

One day, several weeks after his expulsion, I saw him while I stood outside my classroom between classes. Our eyes locked for a moment, and then he disappeared down the stairs at the end of the hall.

Each morning pulling into school, I was alert. I scanned the empty parking lot and the entryway to the building before I got out of the car. Then one morning, driving in, I heard on the radio that a young man, the son of a nurse and a firefighter, had been killed. The police had released his name: Richard T. At school I learned the rest of the story. The shooting was over drugs and a girl: two rival dealers had busted into the room where Richard was having his hair braided. They had shot him twice, once in each eye.

I pull into a parking lot in Worthington, a wealthy suburb of Columbus. I enter a coffee shop, sit down, open my laptop. I write until I run out of time. The cells on my laptop tapped out, the computer threatens to shut down, then it does, before I save a single word. The little green light blinks intermittently. I fold my computer closed, and head home.

C#

A CD of Isaac Stern playing the rapturous music of Béla Bartók's *Violin Concerto No. 2*. As I read the liner notes, an oboe cuts through dark shimmers of string.

Bartók's second violin concerto was the last piece I studied. I'd go to the practice rooms wearing my long coat, violin case in hand, passing the dull brick buildings. At night I'd return using the underground passages, dank and graffiti strewn, my friends echoing solfege at the top of their lungs. The sky was always gray. My head buzzed with scales in perfect fifths, trills, wild leaps to stratospheric pitches, uncharted harmonic territory. Veils of harp. Throbbing heartbeats given to a regiment of basses. A sneering glissando accelerating on a string. Violence gathering in sound at the end of a decade: Bartók completed composition on December 31, 1938.

Earlier I had scanned the CDs on the bookshelves next to my desk. I know them all too well. Schoenberg's *Transfigured Night*, a cello wailed; Beethoven's *Eroica*, clenched fists of chords. No and no. Maybe I've razed too many fields of synapses and should stop listening. Heal up, forget. I grabbed the Bartók.

A slow movement. I can hear Isaiah crying through it, in the background, down the hall. When I hug him before bed each night, he stands holding the wooden bars of his crib like an angelic prisoner. He burrows his head into my chest, rubbing it side to side, telling me, "Stay. Stay. You stay." I cradle his head in my hands until he arches his back. I lower him, slowly, down to sleep.

It is useful, or so I once read in a book on Buddhism, to imagine yourself dead. See your flesh leave your bones. See the whiteness of your bones. Then see the whiteness disintegrate. It is useful to go through the same visualization with family members. Let go of yourself, and of others.

In 1907, Bartók was in love with Stefi Geyer, a violinist, who was nineteen to his twenty-six. He wrote the first concerto, the first movement of which he describes as his confession to her: music written straight from his heart. He was a confirmed atheist, she, a devout Christian. The relationship would not last. Bartók tried to convince her that his position on religion was correct. In one letter, he signed: "Greetings from AN UNBELIEVER." In another: "I sat down at the piano—I have a sad misgiving that I shall never find any consolation in life except in music. And yet..." Bartók then writes a musical quotation containing the first four notes of the concerto, where the violinist plays alone, the orchestra silent. "This is your Leitmotiv."

I stop pushing the lettered keys of my laptop, and push several times instead a button on the CD player to rehear the beginning of the first concerto. I run downstairs to pick out the notes on the piano, ascending: D, F#, A, C#. I hold the C# and listen to it decay. Our front yard is littered with wet leaves that are neither yellow nor orange nor brown. It is November 19, 2002.

ANGEL WINGS

In old days there were angels who came and took men by the hand and led them away from the city of destruction. We see no white-winged angels now.

George Eliot

I've been watching you for the longest time, and I think you're very gorgeous. You don't know who I am, but eventually you will find out. I'm always thinking about you every second, every minute. You're sweet and polite, also very patient. Your beautiful eyes have me hypnotized, so I'm under your spell. By the way, it is not important if you have a boyfriend or not, because that is not going to stop me from liking you. You probably would laugh or freak out when I tell you this, but I've had a crush on you from the first time I saw you. That was about six years ago.

Sincerely,
Manny Ruiz

Driving to school in Bridgeport, I would pass a graffiti-tagged bar before turning right onto Clinton Avenue. I would maneuver around pylons that had been constructed to slow drug traffic. Sneakers, crisscrossed, hung from the wires above me at the light on State Street. Dealers huddled on the corner.

Once, a woman dressed in a white gown soaked with mud and road water approached my car as I waited for the light. She leaned toward my window and smiled, toothless. Behind her, in the window of a Spanish-American store, was a poster of a glistening woman, dark tan, white dress, leaning back against a human-sized bottle of beer. DIOS ES AMOR had been sprayed in dripping blue letters on the brick wall next to her.

I would park in the school lot. Across the street were burned out Victorian-style houses. The activities along the street the school was on had been the target of an F.B.I. investigation, which resulted in the incarceration of several Latin Kings, a number of them my students' relatives. Next to the gutted houses was the elementary school, Elias Howe.

In my classroom, I would remove the sheet metal guard to the radiator and crank a handle. Pipes would bang. Steam would hiss. I would walk to the chalkboard and write the daily quote.

At a little after 5AM, it's raining and windy. I drive to school to pick up *The Old Man and the Sea* before anyone gets in. I'm taking a personal day.

On the board in my suburban classroom I write out a quote for my students:

> "Success is dependent on effort."
> —Sophocles.

See you Monday, I write. I sign my name.

I check email. A parent has written that his son "has a habit of digging a hole for himself early in the school year." *How's he doing?*

It's the fourth week of school. I'm carrying one hundred students, and Kevin is not one who has made any impression on me yet. Normally I can call up an image of any student, like a photograph. Even years later. Should I write back when I'm not supposed to be in school? *Kevin is doing fine. On Monday I'll be returning significant grades, and I'll email you with an update. Thanks for the heads-up.*

I drive to a coffee shop where I eat breakfast and read Hemingway. The old man eats yellow rice. He calls the Portuguese Man of War "agua mala. You whore." The pages are marked with red ink from years ago when I taught in Bridgeport. The students there enjoyed the Spanish text. They knew the meaning and explained it to me.

"Why do you think Hemingway sprinkles Spanish into the text?"

I will show my suburban students the same movie I showed back then. One girl will want to know why the actor playing Santiago has dark skin. "He looks like a monkey," she'll announce. The actor playing Manolin, I'll think to myself, looks like Manny Ruiz. In my classroom I had tacked up his funeral program next to my desk: lean face with a wisp of mustache photocopied on cheap paper.

On Monday, I announce, we will have a reading check quiz.

"The purpose is to see if you've read," I explain. "Nothing deep or analytical. Make sure you know the characters."

I pass back the summer journals and vocabulary. A girl named Hannah writes that *Silas Marner* makes her want to gouge her eyes out. What was George Eliot's problem? Was it a bad childhood? Did she think she was a man? At the end of her response, she writes that she is going to reward herself by eating cake.

Hannah is a quiet one. Dressed in black, wispy blond hair, glasses. She wears a chain with a big, thick lock on it. I find out that she has a twin who decided not to do all the summer reading, and is taking "regular" English. I recruit them for the literary magazine club.

After school, the literary magazine club meets. Thirty students pack their way into my room for the meeting. They are loud. I have to raise my voice to get their attention. We will need a poster to attract submissions, I tell them. I tell them that I entered last year's magazine in a national competition.

"Also, you need to think about ways you would like to change the magazine this year. Maybe you might want to make it thematically related."

Someone suggests we should re-name the magazine. We debate this every year, and every year keep the magazine's name. *The Oracle.*

"Call it JESUS CHRIST!"

"No, no, call it JESUS II, THE RETURN."

"Call it SEPTEMBER ELEVENTH."

"Oh, gee, do you think that would get censored?"

"How about COLUMBINE?

"AL QAEDA!"

"SHIVA!"

In Bridgeport, I didn't have as many students in the literary magazine club, but the energy was the same. The students called the magazine *Truce.* Included were letters to family and friends who had died. One student, Jennifer Diaz, wrote:

> *God bless Manny,*
> *who left us without saying a word.*
> *God bless his family,*
> *for not getting what they deserved.*
>
> *God bless the way you*
> *look at the problems.*
> *God bless the way*
> *you try to solve them.*
>
> *God, bless you*
> *for taking Manny in your hands.*
> *But be careful my Lord—*
> *he is now a man.*

Today: Hemingway. I'll write a definition of allegory on the board. I will draw two circles, one with the letter *A* in it, the other with the letter *B*. I will draw lines connecting *A* to *B*. *A* is "surface meaning." *B* is "below the surface meaning." We will analyze Hemingway's descriptions of Santiago's palms. We will discuss the nail driven through the hand. The image of the mast on his shoulder, the many falls on the way back to the shack.

One may or may not be aided in understanding a text by knowing about the life of the author.

We will watch a video that ends with Hemingway shooting himself, followed by happy clarinet music.

On the way in this morning, I noticed that the cups are still in the fence. Our students use a long stretch of fencing as a message board, filling the holes in the links with white Styrofoam cups. The fence reads: WE MISS YOU SAM HAYES 9-19-03.

It was his heart. Sam was a sophomore. He wasn't my student, and I didn't recognize him when they flashed his picture on the morning announcements. Usually the fence says things like: HAPPY SIXTEENTH BIRTHDAY BRITTANY. Or: GO GIRLS LACROSSE.

The day before Prom, a chime tolls each hour to signify the number of people killed by drunk drivers. Students are encouraged to sign the Prom Promise: they will not drink alcohol. They get a pen if they sign. Students who aren't going to Prom sign just to get the pen.

"What a relief," a student remarks. "Now I won't have to get drunk and have all that promiscuous sex."

The death chime interrupts each hour of the day, even in the middle of class. "There goes another one!" a student exclaims. Then a debate: is it thirty or three hundred people who die each hour, (or is it each second?), because of drunk drivers?

Students are killed each class period by a boy dressed as the Grim Reaper. Black hooded and wearing flip-flops, he shows up during my Honors English class, taps one of my students and hands her a card that she shows me, solemnly. She has been killed by a drunk driver and silenced for the rest of the school day.

In addition to this pre-Prom attempt at fostering student awareness, our administration has also put into place PROJECT WISDOM. Once a week a "wise" saying is read by a model teacher or student over the morning announcement to all homerooms and followed by the tag line: MAKE IT A GREAT DAY OR NOT: THE CHOICE IS YOURS!

Mari ran up to me in the hallway where the baby room was. Some of my students kept their babies in there while they attended classes. Cribs lined the walls. Two white rocking chairs in the center of the room. If I had time, I would go in to visit.

"Mr. Miller, here, look. Recognize anyone?" She shows me a photo, a third grade class. I look at the faces.

"Can't you see which one?"

"No. Show me." She runs her finger across the bottom row and stops on a boy. A chubby boy.

"That's not him."

"That's him."

During my first year in Bridgeport, Manny was one of the most charismatic students I taught. He had the kind of good looks and confidence that made other students look up to him. Girls flirted with Manny. His friends were what some teachers called thugs. For them, school was a joke, a place to meet and to make plans for the gang. They sold drugs. They stole cars for chop shops. A few years later, I would hear that Manny's brother was a player smuggling guns into Bridgeport.

In my class, Manny was always respectful. He knew that I recognized his intelligence.

I remember Irene telling me what happened the first time she'd brought Manny home to meet her mother.

"Are you a gangster?" Irene's mother had asked.

"No," Manny replied.

Irene laughed and told me that her mother thought he was handsome but did not believe him. Manny and Irene seemed pre-ordained. A perfect fit. I kept a copy of the letter he'd asked me to edit. "No mistakes, Miller."

In the cafeteria, a representative from Central Office leads us through a handout to determine if we are highly qualified teachers according to the new federal guidelines. Five steps. Boxes to fill in. We have to write out our daily schedule, and then indicate whether we are qualified to teach it, based on the five steps.

I write that I have a degree in the subject matter that I teach. I sign the back page, tear it off, and give it to our assistant principal. Mickey Mouse gestures wildly at me from his tie.

He had been gone for three weeks, disappeared. Some people said he was on the run because of what he knew.

"Oh, Miller, it was bad. It didn't look like him. They dressed him right, but his skin was yellow and waxy-looking."

"You remember that big snowstorm, right? They picked him up the night it started. They wanted his brother, but couldn't get him. So they got Manny instead. They drove him up 95 and shot him in the back of the head and dumped his body on the side of the highway. He'd been buried under the snow. That's why he was gone so long. They had to wait for all the snow to melt before someone found him."

"Miller, man, I can't take this much longer. Things are getting worse. Manny was a good one. He was like a brother to me."

One teacher said, "He got what he deserved."

Another: "He knew what he was doing, and he knew the consequences. I have no pity for him or his family."

Irene clutched a chain, her face smudged with mascara. She screamed at Mari and Lori: "I'll tell you this—I've got all that little motherfucker's gold. All of it! Fuck him!" They tried to grab her arms.

A tone of self-congratulation pumps loud and clear through the speaker system in the spotless gymnasium. All the teachers from the school system are here, most wearing matching shirts: TAKE THIS JOB AND LOVE IT. The band pounds in, stiff and controlled. The crowd claps with the beat. A leader stands atop a ladder, faces the audience, and salutes. She swivels and catches sight of her mirror image thirty yards to her left. They begin waving time. When the fight song ends, the audience hushes. A seventh grade girls' a cappella choir sings the national anthem in tones as white and pure as angel wings.

A centrally located screen displays graphics and explanations. The state standards for the proficiency tests have been met! All twenty-three of them! Perfect score!

RESPECT + RECIPROCITY = RESULTS. The equation is supported by pictures of different schools and different teachers flashed to different levels of applause. When a popular teacher is flashed, the home school erupts with applause. In several instances, a picture earns only a mild response.

Prepared statements by the union leader are displayed on the screen. The new superintendent plays well to the audience—anecdotes about her retired husband who does, get ready, get this: NOTHING. Laughter.

Another videotaped address—an extended golf metaphor. The game reflects all that we do: choosing the right club, the sand trap that even pros sometimes wind up in, and don't forget to enjoy that perfectly straight drive! The speaker has a club in her hand. The club materializes on stage. The superintendent picks it up and "swings" us into the new year as the speaker system blasts Aretha Franklin singing: R-E-S-P-E-C-T.

CROSSOVER

I grab *The New York Times*, wrapped in orange plastic, off the driveway. It's one of the first frigid December mornings. The cold came late this year. Some of my neighbors left Christmas lights on overnight.

One family on a street down from ours called Hickory Drive, the Stantons—they had a pine tree in their front yard that they used to light up with only blue bulbs. The sight was intoxicating. Before dinner, when it was already dark, I slid underneath the Stanton's tree like a mechanic under a car. The smell of pine mingled with chimney smoke. The snow around me looked blue, as did the green thistles. A darkened bulb in glove, I ran home, hoping that all the other families were at the dinner table and that there had been no witnesses. Once home, I stood beneath our steamed up kitchen window in front of the garage where it was dark. I could hear the quiet snow sifting down around me as I opened my glove to admire the bulb that, like so many others, I'd throw against a hard surface just to hear that distinctive pop.

When I picked up the newspaper, I was thinking about James. I had had a dream about him right before I woke up, one of those dreams that stays with you. We had talked about life after graduation. But James was dead. Killed by a car that had entered the highway going the wrong direction.

I remember him laughing about what his father had said when he was a child: "Boy, you better learn to dribble." He told me how his father had him working a basketball from the time he could walk. James would be short for a basketball player, five-one or two, so he'd better know how to handle the ball.

By the time he was a senior, he was being recruited by a local university. But, academically, James couldn't make it. He used to control the ball well on the court. He would not panic when surrounded by other players more than a foot taller. He could touch the rim. When he would launch a three-point shot, his feet would kick out in front of his body. He would balance in the air like that and somehow heave the ball that looked too big for him to the hoop, and manage to right himself before landing.

After the game James, his girlfriend, and their son would sometimes need a ride. In the bitter cold parking lot, they would bundle into my car, and I would bring them home—a lone strand of Christmas lights framing the door to the apartment, like an unfinished rectangle.

WHAT GOES BEYOND

It was Share Night for the second graders of Indianola Alternative Elementary School. As parents milled about waiting for a show to commence, I waited for Chess Club to end. My son Aidan, who was in first grade at the time, was a member. I had set up shop outside the chess room's door across from a display table on which sticks had been wrapped in string in various ways. A bright red sign with photographs and writing hung above the table. Students had learned about Indonesian culture.

Soon other students would have African drums between their legs. They would imitate the rhythmic patterns tapped, banged, and slapped forth by their teacher. As the drums got louder and louder, the kids' smiles got broader and broader.

I graded compare and contrast essays. Most of my students spelled Hemingway *Hemmingway*. I made red slashes through the extra Ms. One student at the end of her essay quoted a website she had visited:

> Note: I do not support the idea that one person should try to analyze another's work, or try to interpret what the author is saying, this is done in vain, for the only one who truly understands the story is the author. Ernest Hemmingway said: "There isn't any symbolism. The sea is the sea. The old man is an old man. The boy is a boy and the fish is a fish. The shark are all sharks no better and no worse. All the symbolism that people say is shit. What goes beyond is what you see beyond when you know." Ernest Hemmingway, 1952.

She had already brought this up in class. Another had seen it, too. To stave off the rebellion (I had spent a week convincing them that everything was symbolic) I told them to be wary of internet scholars who quoted out of context. I asked her if she remembered the website, and she said no. I wondered if the website had Hemingway with two Ms, or if that was her handiwork. The last sentence seemed mangled.

Of course, I agreed with this out-of-context Hemmingway that "the sea is the sea." But it takes a long life to get that. Two-hundred and twenty-seven pieces of shrapnel removed from one's leg on the Italian Front is useful. Having felt the weight of a fifteen-hundred-pound marlin on the end of one's fishing line is useful. Having cleaned one's own shotgun, the smell of gun oil in one's nose, is useful. My father still cleans the sixteen gauge shotgun he gave to me as a Christmas gift twenty-five years ago. He enjoys that, he tells me over the phone.

I know what he means. There is something satisfying in taking the killing machine apart, looking down the rifled barrel to see black particles that need to be cleaned out. The metal is heavy. The stock can be polished until it gleams.

I search and find the quotation, finally, on a website that summarizes novels and provides critiques and editing services. Harvard students are involved, but the site is "not affiliated with Harvard College." Hemingway is spelled correctly. I email my friend Seb, an English professor, and ask if he knows any Hemingway experts who could check the quote and give me the context. When I see him Saturday at the Unicorn Fall Scholastic Chess Tournament, he says he got the email and one out of the four people he asked will surely ID the quote. Good. I put my headphones back on and return to grading. Periodically there are breaks, and I walk around the school peering into classrooms. Columbus School For Girls. The classrooms are small. One room has only fifteen desks. Newspaper articles tacked into corkboard tell about Muslims. There is a map of Afghanistan. There is a political cartoon making fun of Jesse Jackson, which shows his mouth zipped up and his pants zipper zipped tight. Another board has colored paper cards with "natural highs" written on them. "A nice warm bath" reads one. "Eating ice cream with friends." There are pictures of the girls engaged in academic activities with innocuous looking male teachers. The school's "dietician-developed" menu is available online. In the "atrium" a TV is set up and kids, waiting for pairings to go up, are fed a diet of *Shrek, Jumanji,* and *Searching for Bobby Fischer*, until adults take over and tune in the Ohio State football game.

All morning I grade essays, this time in a place called Mill Street Bagels. It's a dirty place and my wife hates it when I work there because I come back smelling like grease. I like it because it has big tables in the back with halogen bulb lights hung directly above. If I get there during church hours, I have my pick of tables. I'm listening to *Death and the Maiden* while I re-read the comments I wrote next to the Hemingway quote. I scribble out the comment to my student where I wrote that the last sentence might have been written by Hemmingway but surely not by Hemingway. I write that that last sentence was incoherent.

But as I re-read, it seems to make sense: "What goes beyond is what you see beyond when you know." With guilt I scribble out the word "incoherent." I look at the last page of the essay. I have written more red comments around the quote than on any other part of the essay. I stop myself from scribbling out more comments.

I read today that Ken Kesey died. I'm reading the newspaper and the sun is streaming in. After a day of grading, the only things I can remember from the article are that he eventually climbed a mountain without taking LSD, he grew blueberries, and that one of his sons died in a car accident. And I remember the photo of him leaning against the bus he drove cross-country and its name: FURTHER.

In past years, I have worked my symbol and allegory routine on *One Flew Over the Cuckoo's Nest* just like I've done with Hemingway. But now I'm beginning to wonder about the routine itself: what is it based on? What am I teaching my students to do? They already collectively groan when Christ pops up in anything we read. I say that's what happens when you study Western literature. "What about Shiva?" asks one sarcastically. "When are we going to read a story with Shiva in it?"

I hide out in the faculty library in school to work, trying to avoid faculty members. Unfortunately, a former board member is in there using a computer to edit a family video with our tech specialist aiding and abetting. In any case, I hunker down to grade. Then I think I remember seeing the quote in one of those Harold Bloom *Modern Critical Editions.* As I leave the room for the stacks, I hear a horrible rendition of "Hark the Herald Angels Sing," courtesy of the board member's family's Christmas past. I grab two collections, both assembled by Bloom. I should be grading papers, but scan, instead, page after page of commentary. In one interview, Hemingway floats his iceberg principle of writing. He also beats the hell out of the interviewer—each stupid question artfully dodged, each attempt to corner defeated. The question of symbols—for a shining moment I think I'll find the quote—comes up. No quote. Hemingway's revulsion is palpable.

Back in the faculty library again the next day, I copy the following quote from the interview I found yesterday:

> I suppose there are symbols since critics keep finding them. If you don't mind I dislike talking about them and being questioned about them. It is hard enough to write books and stories without being asked to explain them as well.

After school we have a Professional Development Training session on plagiarism. Our AP English teacher leads the session. He loves catching students in the act. He passes out a sample of a student essay and explains how he honed in on the phrase "celestial nihilism"—*way too sophisticated for our kids.* Using one of his favorite search engines, he locates the passage. *Bingo. Nailed'em.* Later that night, following suit, I find the quote and the following source:

> Ernest Hemingway (1899–1961), U.S. author. Letter, 13 Sept. 1952, to the critic Bernard Berenson (published in *Selected Letters*, ed. by Carlos Baker, 1981), of *The Old Man and the Sea*, published that year.

I find the *Selected Letters* in the local library while Aidan finds "the scariest" *Goosebumps* movie. Later, with the baby watching a "Barney Christmas Special" and son number two, Elias, entranced as well, I sit at the top of the steps scanning the letters in search of September 13, 1952. Berenson, I read in the introduction, is "an octogenarian art historian." Hemingway, in his letter to the older man, brings up a book of the war years, his wife, Homer, *Moby-Dick*, the ocean, a request for a blurb for *The Old Man and the Sea*, and hurricane weather. And, of course he states that the "boy is a boy and the fish is a fish." This after the claim that the ocean is like a whore: one you can't love, but can know well, and continue to "go around with" even after she infects you.

WATERCOLOR

Two seagulls hover above the ferry to Seattle. The sky has a bit of cloud cover: gray-white, with blue that peeks from behind. A dark green tree line gently slopes.

Hands hold bread for seagulls. I am riding a ferry with my father, who has been staying at the VA hospital. I am returning to the airport to fly home. The doctors had removed part of a lung and stapled his chest closed. Also: a quintuple bypass.

Another man is with us. He used to be a Hell's Angel. He fought in the Vietnam War. He and a third buddy picked me up at the airport and drove me to see my father. They called it their getaway car. The buddy did not speak much. His room at the VA was spotless. Within six months, he would die there.

Jeff. The Hell's Angel's name is Jeff, and he gets a big kick out of how the seagulls come down and take the bread from his hand. "Get a load of this." Jeff has a son he has not seen in some time. The son lives with his mother in another state, a southern state, North Carolina maybe. My father will die two years later from this day, in South Carolina. Jeff will have planned to stop by to visit, on the way to see his son.

Jeff tells me, the night I arrive, how much the visit means to my father. He says it helped him make it through surgery. Later that night, we all pack into the getaway car and go to the supermarket. We buy bags of potato chips and pretzels. My father imitates Peter Sellers playing the part of Inspector Clouseau: we will bring it back to our "room." He uses the words "Pope" and "bomb." He wants me to do my imitation of Bill Murray in *Caddyshack*. I try my best, but it has been twenty years since I did it for him. I mumble a few words. The roads are dark outside the car as we head back to the VA.

In the room at the VA, there is a watercolor my father has been working on, based on a photograph of my parents' house in Connecticut. A one-story brown house, flowers bursting with color all around the yard. My other father—the man who married my mother, adopted me, and raised me as his own—has taken to gardening as a way of expressing himself. There isn't much else he can do. My parents commissioned the work from my father out of charity.

I visit my father in the morning. When he comes out of the bathroom, his white robe opens and I see the staples and the wasted body. He lights a cigarette. We go into town to get breakfast at a place that has good bacon and eggs. We walk down on the wharf and look at the boats he used to draw. He's off in a fantasy about how, with a little money, he could deck one of those boats out, live on it, catch salmon.

It was my first year teaching in Ohio when I found out about the surgery. I had to miss school for a couple of days, and so I took my students' essays to grade. At the VA, I got to stay for free in an empty room. Like my father's room, its walls were close enough together that it seemed they might crush a sleeper in the night. But I could crack open a window and get some light. The air smelled good: clean, fresh, natural. I understood why he had returned to the Northwest. It wasn't only that he trusted the doctors. I zipped up my black leather coat, grabbed my sunglasses, and walked down the path to see if he was up.

Down at the dock there was a totem pole: large, eight or nine feet high. One of the heads had a beak.

At night, we ate dinner at a Chinese restaurant, and my father recalled the first time he had visited me. At the time, I had been house sitting in Connecticut. He had driven from California in the orange Datsun. His dog, Patch, was with him then. The story he loved to remember was about the pond next to this house. He had picked up a rock to see if he still "had it," and he threw it far out past the center. I picked up a rock and launched it over the center of the pond, beyond the ripples that his rock made, and onto the far shore.

A GREATER MONSTER

THE WAY I SEE IT

Lejana tierra mía
Bajo tu cielo,
Quiero morirme un día
Con tu consuelo
Y oir el canto de oro
De tus campanas
Que siempre añoro;
No sé si al contemplarte al regresar
Sabré reir o llorar. [1]

"Lejana Tierra Mía"; music by Carlos Gardel; lyrics by Alfredo Le Pera; recorded by Editions CMG in New York, March 19, 1935

1

It was a job. I didn't want to pick peaches, because that was hot work. If you've ever picked peaches in the hot sun you will remember that peach fuzz comes off and gets in your clothes, and it is just like itching powder and drives you crazy. So instead of doing that, I joined the J. Lipp Sullivan Funeral Home in Marysville, California. It was the one funeral home in town. Mr. Sullivan kindly gave me a job and let me work with the embalmers. I got to drive the first car, which is the car you go out in first when you don't know if you have a dead person or a still-alive person. And if the person happens to be dead then you have to drive back and get the funeral car—you can't haul stiffs in the first called car. We'd go over there and try to sell them an expensive casket—that's what the call is for—if they are going to die. If we could, if he were on his last legs, they'd want to make arrangements in advance and we'd sell them outrageously expensive funerals. The cost of the casket covered everything else. I even got

[1] *O distant earth of mine,/Under your sky,/I yearn, one day, to die--/Only you can console me./I long to hear again/The golden song,/Tolled forth from your bells./As I contemplate you and my return,/Upon returning,/I don't know if I'll laugh or cry.* trans. author

to sing sometimes. They'd pay me an extra five dollars. I remember I sang for a black man who had died, an old man. I can't remember the song.

> January 8, 1961. I haven't written for a long time. Been doing things of no import, making money. Now don't flip—I'm in Hollywood. I left New York to make a penny in motion pictures. People say I am good and can be sold. Went to Warner Bros. and read a scene from *The Caine Mutiny*. There is a lot of money out here, and there are a lot of people trying to get it. Funny, me too. It's because of my son. I'm gone from him now. Someday, he will know how much I love him. I must leave him. I must do these things. I don't know any other way.

The sky was gray. Stopped at an intersection, I watched as a helicopter landed in the distance on the other side of the river. The light changed. I drove north. On the radio, Garrison Keillor intoned. It was the birthday of a writer who got a twenty-minute trial and was executed in Moscow. It was the birthday of a poet who wrote:

> The water-lilies on the meadow stream
>   Again spread out their leaves of glossy green;
> And some, yet young, of a rich copper gleam,
>   Scarce open, in the sunny stream are seen,
> Throwing a richness upon Leisure's eye,
>   That thither wanders in a vacant joy;

The poet had made paper out of birch bark. He had made ink. He had suffered from visions of spirits and demons. He had escaped once from an asylum, only to be returned.

> September 13, 1963. I did not go insane. I'm in the Rijksmuseum and have just finished a cheese sandwich and a Coke. If I find this so satisfying, I must be insane. Who are the insane? Institutions do not house the insane, only the sick. I am going to paint again. I have just finished a painting. It is green. It is the end of the sunlight in the trees and leaves. It is the beginning of itself. And I am going to paint more. I may paint still life. To see these great Dutch still life for real is almost too much. How insane were they? They painted grapes. To paint a grape is to prove one's insanity.

In the children's section of a bookstore, Isaiah played with a train set while I read a magazine. On the inside cover, a post-MFA program was advertised for writers who wanted to secure teaching credentials. *Pragmatic. Realistic.*

A few years ago, in a writing seminar at Ohio State, after the class had work-shopped an MFA student's memoir excerpt, the professor had added: "And we'll all look back when this is published as a wonderful book and remember how we first read it here." Quotations about art, literature, and music had been written in calligraphy on the walls of the seminar room. *I write music as a sow piddles. —Mozart.*

Another magazine had a picture of a starlet on the cover. Norman Mailer was interviewed. Mailer said he liked Allen Ginsberg, but that Ginsberg had been a nut sometimes. The woman next to me commented that the bookstore ought to provide more comfortable chairs. Her blond-haired child played with the trains. The boy pressed a button. A whistle blew, and a train chugged.

When I was a boy, I used to go with my mother to the Saugatuck train station to pick up my father who commuted to New York. He worked in advertising. I would step close to the edge of the platform and peer down the length of the tracks.

The conductors gave me punched tickets. Waves of heat radiated off the tracks in the distance. The sound of steam when a train arrived. Squealing brakes. Doors would open and commuters would step down, car after car, until the platform surged with quick steps and hurry.

My father would have a gift: a pen light, a key chain, a tiny compass. If not, he'd give me a lifesaver. When trains flashed through the station, non-stop towards New York, I'd see how close I could get. The windows, doors, metal rushed by—a heavy CLICKCLICK CLICKCLICK CLICKCLICK on the tracks.

In the barbershop in Worthington, the walls were covered with pictures of sports figures, team flags, football helmets. Each item was autographed. In one black-and-white photo a hunter pulled up the head of a buck. Two TVs were mounted above the long seat cushion. Piles of magazines for men. The TVs were either tuned to sports or the country music station. By the door there stood a seven-foot cardboard cutout of a basketball player. The floor was covered with hair.

My barber, Timmy, was upset. His dark brown eyes watered. He was unshaven. He said he had lost it on his nine-year-old son that morning because the boy had taken his bike around the corner without asking, and *there were nut-jobs out here.*

"Even across the street, a guy just held up a bank."

"Mmm," I said.

Shaking his head in disgust, he added that his wife's mother was stabbed to death. Timmy saw a lot of different people coming through his door each day. He said he was not judging people who walked into his shop, he was *discerning.* He repeated the word, bowed low, spread his arms out.

"People walk in here and I can see it on their face: anger. Or worse: arrogance. The way I see it—and believe me it isn't pretty—people turn a corner early in their lives, real early, start drinking in high school, say, or doing drugs. And people have no love. Where's the love? *Come on.* And what happens when you have no love? Just look at London and the bombs. *Come on.* Husbands cheating and beating their wives, drinking and driving, drugs. I see it every day, right here. Just look at the TV." A breaking story flashed across the screen—a thirteen-year-old girl had been abducted in the parking lot of a local mall.

"See what I mean?"

I nodded.

Before I left, Timmy spun me around and asked me what I thought.

My father's voice says, *I was always uncomfortable in the presence of death.* He says this slowly. His voice is lower pitched than in real life, because I have slowed the speed of the tape with the help of the transcription machine.

I didn't enjoy working with dead folks. But there were good times. Much better than the peaches. And I lived at the place, upstairs, over the embalming room, over the caskets. Of course there was no air-conditioning back then. The dead people were placed in refrigerated areas, so it didn't smell like that. But I still can't stand the smell of embalming fluid to this day. Anyway, I'd invite people to come up. I had one semi-girlfriend who was going to become a nurse. She thought she wanted to go into the army as a W.A.C. or the navy as a W.A.V.E. So I invited her into the place to see one of the bodies. When I whipped back the sheet, she fainted. She decided after that she was not going to become a nurse.

In a letter to his dying father, Leopold, Mozart writes: "As death, when we come to consider it closely, is the true goal of our existence, I have formed during the last few years such close relationships with the best and truest friend of mankind that death's image is not only no longer terrifying to me, but is indeed very soothing and consoling, and I thank God for graciously granting me the opportunity...of learning that death is the key which unlocks the door to our true happiness. I never lie down at night without reflecting that—young as I am—I may not live to see another day. Yet no one of all my acquaintances could say that in company I am morose or disgruntled."

> November 27, 1963. Morning. No painting yet. It is cold today. I have lived my life as I have seen fit—unfit in most cases. But I won't get a chance to make a change. Even in death. When will it end? I almost look for it. Yet I go on living. I find no fear in death. It could be a sleep I have long waited for, almost to the point of being careless.

At 7AM I played tennis with an ophthalmologist on his peeling court. Drew was a stout man, bearded, sandy-haired. He had a jovial, easy-going demeanor. As I walked into the kitchen that opened into the den, I saw a teenager sprawled on a couch. "The kids love this place—I don't even know who that is. My son's friends just crash here."

Drew wore reading glasses when we played quartets—he could play violin, viola, and he was learning piano. He sailed. He took tennis lessons. He wrote fiction and nonfiction. Once he gave me a chapter of a novel that began in a rainforest. After tennis, he would hand me a thirty-page essay about his passion for sailing and the long-standing conflict with his father, a minister. Ten to twenty eye surgeries a day provided the means.

On the court, Drew hit a hard forehand, the product of years of drills. He disliked playing me because my shots were unorthodox. But he rationalized: "It's good for me. I told my pro about it." Drew explained the correct approach to returning cuts, in terms of ball speed, angles, body position.

The baselines of the court were eroded in spots, which made calls of "in" or "out" approximations. Cracks and ridges on both sides of the net required careful navigation to avoid injury. Walking back to the house, we stepped around the half-built deck and carefully tread on mossy stone. The pool looked like a small pond.

In the kitchen, Drew told me about an educational book project he had sent to an agent. He was certain he could teach people to read German with 50% comprehension in one hour, 100% comprehension in thirty hours. He added that he had written a forty-page paper on cognition. He had learned all the neuroscience there was on cognition—it didn't take long, we just don't know that much about it, we don't even know where memory is located.

Mr. Sullivan did not work there. He was the owner and a very wealthy man because of the business. But he had an embalmer, and the embalmer needed help. I would not actually participate in the embalming, except that I would prepare the body. You wash him down and make certain that the blood flows down through the thing in the table so that it goes into the waste thing. Nor did I do any cosmetic work afterward, nothing like that, but I did sell caskets, and I did sing. Sometimes I'd throw water-filled balloons out of the upstairs window on people who were passing by. They thought that could never happen in front of a funeral home, so they couldn't imagine where it came from. I threw it. But you had to have lighter moments.

The phone rang. I picked up. A female voice said, "I have great news for you. Due to the new cable increases…"

2

For a few days I had gone to the soccer fields at the bottom of The Park of Roses, set up a chair, and read Chatwin's *The Songlines* under the sun. A dragonfly hovered like a vibrating needle. Bees climbed white clover near my bare feet. Thus I avoided the act of transcribing my father's audiotape. I planned to see *Romeo and Juliet* at Schiller Park with Seb and his family later in the week. Some of my former students would be there. In an email Seb said the sword fights were good, Mercutio died well, and the moon made an appearance.

Each night, Aidan practiced the Gigue from Bach's *Partita in B-flat*. The patterned notes on the page looked like a scroll of hieroglyphs. As the marks were interpreted, one hand crossed back and forth over the other: the left hand flicked a quarter note above the right hand, then the right hand played a two note eighth-note pattern, then the left hand crossed back down to the lower part of the keyboard for more quarter notes. The left hand carried on a conversation with itself over the span of keys. The right interjected a chirped commentary throughout: Klee's *Twittering Machine* brought to life.

I drove to Starbucks. With my coffee and book, I sat at a window-side table. At the end of the hall, a door opened, and an employee walked out: twenties, earring, short hair.

Chatwin described a woman made attractive by awkwardness in her movements.

I watched two women walk to the counter, get their orders and leave. The first was tall and skinny. Her legs were muscular. As she quickly slipped into her square-shaped car, the muscle flexed around her shoulder blades. Above the bumper of her car, in silver letters: ELEMENT. The woman was in a hurry, her face pinched.

The second woman—younger, blonde, short, stood at the counter. Her rounded calves came to attention when she stood at the counter.

Our study was on the second floor. The walls had built-in bookshelves and a window that looked out onto the road. Two desks. Two laptops. I grabbed the book C was reading and flipped it open to the first page: "If Enlightenment Man stands discredited as gendered and ethnocentric, then the individual has become a contested category." Enlightenment Man, I imagined, was big, filled with a light that emanated from eyes and ears, even from the top of his head. But to no avail. Further down, the concept of identity was linked to geography and space.

> November 11, 1963. I went to the Hilton and had a great time. Met Errol Garner the jazz pianist and Kelly his drummer, and Mr. Calhoun—can't remember his first name—the Big Bass man in the trio. We had a ball till 4AM. When I came home, I was sick as a dog. Two days later, feeling a little better. So alone and no light except what might be considered will power. I need to find some way to concentrate. I hope I can overcome these things, so they won't get too far into my painting. But I won't know until that time I paint again. It is impossible to sleep, so I have nights and days to contend with until it happens. The only thing I can do is make a mental effort to shorten the time and keep myself together. Then I can begin with full strength.

The cup of coffee I had brought home, read:

The Way I See It #37

Embrace this right now life while it's dripping, while the flavors are excellenty woesome. Take your bites with bravery and boldness since the learning and the growing are here in these times, these exact right nows. Capture these times. Hold and kiss them because it will soon be very different.

Jill Scott Musician. Her songs can be heard On Starbucks Hear MusicTMstation, XM Satellite Radio Channel 75.

This is the author's opinion, not necessarily that of Starbucks. To read more or respond, go to www.starbucks.com/wayiseeit.

Over the D Street bridge over the Feather River between Yuba City and Marysville, they had built a new bridge, and they had left some stanchions from the old bridge in the water—the rods that supported the cement were still coming out from them. One night, a drunk fell off the bridge and landed head first on one of these things. It went in on the top of the head and wound up in his stomach. He was there, upside-down. And it drew a tremendous crowd to see this poor man in this condition. Because it was my job, I had to pull him off. I did this by lassoing both legs and having somebody help me. Of course when he came off, everything inside him had turned to jelly and flew out. In my position, as a man doing this, I had authority, which I had lacked in previous times.

For lunch, I drove down to the campus to pick up C. We needed to make a list of things to pack. On the way up, I saw workmen smashing down the gym. One of the walls had a punched-out hole through which I could make out what had been a pool. Pedestrians stopped and stared.

We went to the North Market. At a picnic table in the front of the building, we determined the order of rooms to pack.

It looked like rain. C dropped me at a place closer to home.

Caribou, like Starbucks, was over-air-conditioned. It smelled like drying glue and polyurethane. I sat in a black leather chair across from the fire. The glass in front of the lapping flames was cold. Nearby sat a teenage boy with two girls. He told them, "I'm wearing a girl's shirt." Then one of the girls sang a song she said she loved. The singing girl tied a plastic wrapper around the boy's finger.

I was at the point in the book where Chatwin and Volchok have the following exchange:

> "So a musical phrase is a map reference?"
>
> "Music," said Volchok, "is a memory bank for finding one's way about the world."
>
> "I shall need time to digest that."
>
> "You've got all night," he smiled. "With the snakes!"

As I walked home in the drizzle, I heard in my head a passage from "Dance of the Sugarplum Fairies." I had heard it as a child. The device that played the music had been red and white, and as it played, a filmstrip would pop up, one frame at a time projected on a screen, to a beep. A green Christmas tree, boxes all around. A white mouse. Submerged in darkness with the rest of the room, I stood and stared.

The music was an X on a map: my parents' house, near the bottom of the sledding hill, just below Mr. Reilley's house with the white garage, where thirty-six years ago Gary would bang his drum set—infuriating my father. A door in the garage had led to an office in which Mr. Reilley had kept a .38 caliber handgun in a desk drawer.

Back then, I used to listen to older children yelling in the night. They played flashlight tag, and I stood on my bed and watched the lights in the backyard.

The cicadas in waves and the fan set on low, I imagined a mad scientist who made heat lightning that flashed the tree line into relief. I watched him pull the lever of an electrical machine, his laboratory equipped like the one in Frankenstein's castle. Voltage cracked and popped. His lab was housed in a warehouse beyond Hickory Drive. He controlled the weather.

Every night, I would sit in a trance. I would travel to view the warehouse, or to observe neighborhood battles, which I orchestrated from above. The world below was spread in a grid, and I would follow streets, looking down on treetops, until I hovered above my elementary school and its tar roof, and landed on the kickball field.

Some nights, I would see a spade-tipped tail slither by the bedroom door in the yellow light. I would try to call my father. The effort to speak would cause me to spiral into darkness. At the bottom, I knew, I would face him, the one I approached in nightmares but never faced.

"You are going to have to kill me," I would say. But I could not speak. A curtain came down.

In the afternoons, I daydreamed and rode the falling pitch of propeller planes as they flew to Sikorsky Airport.

Linda, who waited tables at PJ's Pancake House, typed papers for me when I was in college. In the spring of 1983, she opened the door to her small apartment and showed me in. She lit a cigarette, and the walls tightened around us. I admired her collections. Linda wanted me to hear something. She placed a record on the turntable and lowered the needle. A light hiss, and then Bach played on an organ: music rolled, twisted, spiraled. Taking a quick drag, Linda turned to me. It was as if she had inhaled flame, as if when she exhaled, she would incinerate the apartment. She looked away. "Can you hear the anger?"

I got a call from somebody way out in the country. A man had gone to sleep under his tractor and not put it in gear and it ran over him. He was still alive, so we went in the ambulance. Driving the ambulance was a big thing to me. I sped through town with the siren blaring and the lights and everybody got out of my way. I had one hell of a time. Well, we picked him up. The poor man was in agony and I was not prepared to do anything for him. I was not allowed to do anything for him. So it was twelve miles driving with this guy in the back of the ambulance screaming in absolute agony.

In the introduction to Chatwin's *In Patagonia*, Nicholas Shakespeare recounts meeting Bruce Chatwin. Chatwin said wild stories came to him when he was in Patagonia—he did not have to seek them out. He thought it might have to do with the wind.

Last night, the statue of Schiller looked away from the play. It stared west toward the sun, which set behind bright-rimmed clouds. Beams of light shot into the blue sky. My students came. They sat on blankets, exchanged treats, and laughed when they saw women had been given codpieces. Even Escalus was a Princess.

3

For three days in August, I stayed at my in-laws', in Philadelphia. I had to train in their office to work as a salesperson. I'd make just enough money while we lived at the Institute for Advanced Study. C, a visiting scholar, would write her book, and I'd get more time to write than when I was teaching. I'd send manuscripts out. The Institute was on a 500-acre natural preserve. The grounds had many paths to walk, to take in the beauty. The apartments were designed by a Bauhaus architect. C's office would be on Einstein Drive. C would decide, during that year, that she was no longer in love with me. It would take two years for that thought, like this narrative, to drag itself into view.

My in-laws' company arranged concert tours for string quartets, soloists, trios, dance companies, and the like. The first day a nightmare woke me at 6AM. I drove into town to get coffee and read before the workday started.

That morning, as music pumped out of a speaker from above my head, I read the part in *The Songlines* where a man is bitten in the face by a snake that had wrapped itself around the axle of a car. A golden retriever waited patiently outside the store. My mind wandered to the work ahead: one group emigrated from Taiwan in 1982. Another championed the work of living composers and had been featured in a GAP ad. A string quartet had played music for the last Olympics ("...that music about water—say that, people love it, works like a charm").

Selling is the ability to say the right words in the right order at the right time. For three days I read flyers, biographies, and reviews of the artists and compiled pitch points on 3x5 cards.

After the training, my father-in-law drove me to the airport. The setting on the up-ramp to departing flights was bleak: warehouses, concrete, gas tanks. I saw myself standing next to an empty warehouse. I put a gun to my head and pulled the trigger. The body dropped without sound. A silent movie. Herons, like splinters of white, stood stiff in the marsh.

My father told me he would fly drunk all the way to the Orient to keep his nerves at bay—back when he traveled to places like the Philippines and China. Flying didn't bother me much. Once I had flown over squares of white fields, anxiety riddled, and had wished for a crash. I was twenty-two.

A month after, back at college, I read Frost's:

> And lonely as it is that loneliness
> Will be more lonely ere it will be less—
> A blanker whiteness of benighted snow
> With no expression, nothing to express.

During the flight, I read more Chatwin. He had compiled selections from notes he'd kept in Moleskins. The girl next to me read Márquez, and I remembered reading *Love in the Time of Cholera* as C and I took the bus ride to Salta and Jujuy. In Buenos Aires where we had lived, I walked by the street peddlers and the smell of burnt peanuts; corner flower stands overflowed with clusters of red, violet, yellow; newsstands flew baby blue Argentine flags, pictures of Diego Maradona the soccer star, and Carlos Saúl Menem, *El Presidente*, in a yellow suit, slick black hair, Wolfman Jack sideburns with shocks of white; at the zoo, a lion starved like a dog on a mound of dirt, a panther passed out in cage, a giraffe choked to death on a bottle top; ghosts of European architects and the whiteness of *el obelisco* set against the sky—*azul*; I'd pass the frenzy of the black market and hyper-inflation to the American library, where I read the poetry collection from the 1950s: Berryman, Sexton, Plath; I kept a key chain that played the Peronist National Anthem; we raced elevators between brown-outs; a trip to Patagonia ended in Bariloche and a room rented by an old German woman with black-and-white pictures from Deutschland; for the first time, I read *Moby-Dick*.

On the way to a going-away party for a former student, I stopped in a bookstore to pick up a present: a CD of Nina Simone, 1966. I signed the card, and as I walked to the car, someone waved to me from inside an SUV. The car stopped. It was a former student, Kalpana Sundarajan, whose last name had changed to Sundar by senior year. She jumped out and we hugged. She was preparing to head to college, trying to get her books ahead of time for a course on Indian and English literature. She told me that she had seen a novel by Gogol—the name of the protagonist from a novel I had given her. I explained to Kalpana's mother, the driver, that I would be living in Princeton for the next year.

"I asked Kalpana to apply to Princeton, but she didn't. A friend of mine's daughter got in—*a very good water polo player*."

I drove to a complex of houses called Briarwood, or Brookside. At the fork, I was uncertain. Everything looked the same. By luck, I ran into Erin's street.

Dressed in black, Erin's mother greeted me at the door, happy I could come. She offered me champagne. Downstairs, in the finished basement (drum set, electric guitars, walls decorated with movie posters), the girls had pierced lips, tongues, eyebrows. Erin's older sister, visiting from NYU, played with her lip, rolling a metal bar on her tongue. She was going to major in art history and spend next summer in Prague.

Later that night, Erin handed me a small silver ball.

I rolled the tiny ball in my palm.

"You can have that driven into the skin of your forehead, if you want to be cool."

The day before we left for Princeton, I walked towards High Street, Chatwin stored next to my laptop. Across from the top of our street was a Jiffy Lube; to the left a Wendy's with the ad: FOLLOW YOUR GUT INSTINCT AND ORDER A CLASSIC TRIPLE. A few yards south on High Street, and I slipped into a used-book store, one that had been there for thirty years. Old books: Bible stories illustrated by Gustave Doré—Cain holds a club aloft; a child drowns in the deluge. A brief note was included inside a special edition of *Silas Marner* printed in London. The editor recalled reading the book in 1907, and then again in 1952. His views had changed.

In one anthology, I found the story of John Clare's escape and his four-day walk home. Classical music played as I read. The bookshelves were tall, the passage between them narrow. When I inquired about Clare, there was no database, no idea, really, what was in stock. Diaries, collected letters. Heavy pages. Clare was there. When he had escaped from the asylum, I knew he would have headed home. I hoped, too, to find the lily pad poem on old paper. I thought of the prehistoric lily pads I had rowed around at summer camps called Indian Walk and Singing Oaks.

Growing up, the Indians we had heard most about were the Pequots. In nearby Southport, the Pequot Library. On the Post Road, Pequot Liquors and the Pequot Motel—a wretched strip of rooms that was eventually replaced by the Pequot Landing Luxury Townhouses. Westport would become the home of the super-wealthy. (The one-story house I grew up in, which my parents bought in 1966 for $26,000 was recently appraised at $650,000. Developers wanted to buy it, raze the house, and rebuild.)

Meanwhile, the descendants of the indigenous people of Connecticut got a license to run gambling casino resorts on I-95, a couple of hours north.

4

The first conference I attended as a booking agent for Richter Artists Management was held in Albuquerque, New Mexico. You could walk the streets of that city and have no idea that it nestles beneath a range of mountains. After spending a day inside the convention center—each room the size of an aircraft hangar—I went for a jog and ran west on Tijeras. I outran Wendy's, Kentucky Fried Chicken, McDonald's. I jogged by a complex of white condominiums called The Castle. The street quieted down, till I heard the sound of my shoes padding the ground. Middle-class houses gave way to adobe-like apartments, then a trailer park.

During a lunch break, I sat on a bench outside the center. The sun was hot, the air, dry. It felt like the Colonial Northwest of Argentina: sun, sky, and an altitude that framed all objects—the ornate Catholic church, the Spaniard on a horse made of red stone, the one-story white buildings, the guard with his machine gun—with vertiginous perfection. Departing a colonial town at night, the bus drove for deserted miles, while we stared out the windows into blackness. Once I saw lines of fire burning in the dark hills. At a rest stop, a dog came up to beg, its right eye swollen as big and black as an eight ball.

But Albuquerque, with its tall buildings, its major chain hotels, its convention center, tried to be an American city. A few feet away, a lizard: body alert, head raised like an artist's depiction of a miniature dinosaur. It was thin, long as a pen, and shimmered with spectrum. Its tail was a backward C.

At night I heard a string quartet play an arrangement of a Duke Ellington tune. All four players rose out of their seats on cue several times during the performance. Then they settled back down. The first violinist told a story about a Tango competition in which the quartet had won prizes. They had played an arrangement of a Carlos Gardel song. "Even to this day," the violinist said, "fresh flowers are on his grave, although he has been dead for seventy years."

In another carpeted exhibition room, a Patsy Cline imitator was decked out as a glittering cowgirl. I found a seat. Now a tall bearded man wearing round glasses took the stage: an Alaskan fiddler who recited poems and told a story about visiting Eek, Alaska. He said that a song about a chicken laying eggs had changed his life.

Before the Alaskan fiddler began his twenty-minute allotted show time, he drew a map in the air with his fiddle-bow. He traced his journey from Alaska down to Florida, to Chicago, and then *here*: Albuquerque, New Mexico.

Then he performed the song that changed his life. That song was what had made him take the journey. At several points, he stopped playing and made the sound of the hen: QUA! QUA! QUA!

When I had run out of the city, a local in the hotel gym later told me, I had run over the Rio Grande. The river was low, and the water was mud colored. I'd been jogging on Interstate 66. On the other side of the river, in the distance: mesas, like half-note rests for the setting sun.

The next morning, in the lobby gift shop, I bought glass stones carved with petroglyphs of the sun and whirlpool; two toy animal lizards, yellow and red; and a t-shirt with an image of Kokopelli. I read on the card that Kokopelli, the hunchbacked flute player, "is probably best known for music he played on his flute. He brought warmth and life to both people and the land. His image, which can represent travel and adventure, was carved upon canyon walls and desert rocks. In his hunchback, he carried the seed of plants and flowers." I copied these words on the only paper available, the inside cover of *The Songlines.* Just below, it says, "Chatwin died outside Nice, France, on January 17, 1989."

5

To get in, I had to wait in line. I then had to descend, slowly, into the red tunnel. A couple in the line discussed how creepy (or not creepy) Gene Wilder was. At the bottom, a woman escorted me to my seat. I took out a pad and paper and someone asked me if I were a reviewer.

The bassist strolled in, purposeful, picked up his bass and pulled cable-thick strings, pitches deep in the jazz that played through speakers directly in front of my face. An old and dented sousaphone, tarnished brass in a circle, was mounted on a wall.

A blonde-haired woman wearing red rain gear stood in the doorway. Bill came over. Just below my table, a group of twenty settled in. They all spoke a foreign language. After drinks had gone around, the room got louder.

As I looked up from my notebook, I saw a line of white keys. A guitar strummed through speakers.

The black-suited drummer wore a pink tie: a pattern of diamonds. On stage, the tie turned orange. A few drum rolls, and he left.

The drummer returned. He took the high-hat stand apart, wrapped tape at a midpoint—TAP TAP TAP—and tightened a silver screw, oblong in shape. He tested each drum. He whisked brushes on a cymbal, then left again.

A man in his twenties, large and masculine, was with his date. An ideogram had been tattooed onto his forearm. They sat next to me.

Light flooded the stage: red velvet. The trio walked in to applause. Harmonic tuning like whale song. TAP TAP. Seated, Bill turned to the audience and said: "We will commence with a piece by Al McKibben. This is 'Simplicity.'"

A subway rumble at the end of Shearing's "Enchanted." During a drum solo, the man's date lengthened her hair out with her hands to the end of a curl. Her black shoes came to points.

"Liza."
"Somebody Loves Me."
"I Was So Young, You Were So Beautiful."

The second set started at eleven.

The man shrugged. He ordered the date to finish her drink: "Finish it."

"I think it's still raining out."

Another couple replaced the first. A Japanese man took their photo. They returned the favor. The Japanese man knelt in front of the drum set.

In the back room, Bill ate sushi and the bassist and drummer listened to a baseball game. I sat on a cardboard box. Bill ran through a sheaf of tunes—a few notes on paper with chords. Two pieces were in B-flat, too close together.

During the second set, water dripped from the ceiling onto the drummer's cymbal. He stopped from time to time, turned, grabbed a towel, and sopped it up.

At the end of the evening, Bill grabbed his coat and his hat, and we headed out. The street reflected city lights.

6

December 6, 2005. Smoke puffed from the laundry room stacks across the yard. The computer screen was hard to see—I was snow-blind from the walk in the woods. Beethoven's *Bagatelles* played on the CD player. I had brought the disc in, frosted from being in the car, wiped it on my shirt, and put it in. The pianist Alfred Brendel, scarf draped around his neck, looked out from behind a window through thick glass frames.

Next to the liner notes was a lithograph of Beethoven wearing top hat and tails. He grasps a concert program behind his back and looks into the distance.

I followed a trail that led toward the sun. It didn't take long until all signs of the Institute were obscured by trees. Animal tracks and boot marks cluttered the path. Geese honked overhead, and a woodpecker tapped. Small clumps of snow fell from trees.

Farther on, I saw someone in the distance, walking with dogs. I stopped where a tree had fallen and hung suspended in the path.

Finally, I came to a snow-covered suspension bridge. No one had been on it since the previous night's snowfall. I climbed up on it and heard a creak. I crouched. Feathers of snow fell and landed on the river. They didn't disappear immediately. Instead, they turned to flakes of icy skin. They made circles expand into other circles. I stayed in a crouch on the bridge, holding its steel cables for balance. Snow blew around me like white ash.

On the way back, I took a different path. Sun at my back, a wave of light washed over the trees, rolling through them like scales in the *Bagatelles.*

Bill called, and I read to him some of the liner notes. In one of the *Bagatelles,* Beethoven broadens the register to give the sense that the theme is being explored from a new perspective.

"That's total bullshit. Don't believe that crap."

He told me the only thing you need to know about Beethoven is that he was stone cold fucking deaf.

The sun cut a diagonal across the computer screen.

Before the walk in the woods, I had dropped Isaiah at the Institute's pre-school. I stood for a while with a teacher.

"He's really been getting into his artwork," she said.

"He probably comes by that naturally. My biological father—I say biological because I didn't really know him—was an artist."

"Well, we have something in common then—I didn't know my father either. He was an actor. He died when I was two. Suicide."

I didn't tell her my biological father was an actor, too. He had acted to make money so he could paint. A few minutes on the computer using his stage name, and I found the following:

> "OUTLAWS" TV SERIES 1960-1962. "CHARGE AKA OUTPOST" EPISODE #2.23-22 MARCH 1962. CHRISTOPHER KING AS MYLES REE. "THE HERO" NOVEMBER 1966 EPISODE #1.8 "THE DAY THEY SHOT SAM GARRETT"

Before CB, my biological father, died, he told me he had painted one self-portrait.

> October 11, 1963. The last few days I have not been painting. I have been suffering from an acute case of major depression. It came about in such a

> minor way it was difficult to realize what was going on. It has been physical as well as mental to the point where I've been acting like an animal of the lowest order. I am lonely. I have started a self-portrait. If I can finish it, it will be the first conclusion. I may turn to people, or I may stay with still life. In an hour I am going to the police station to check in. That is a step in the right direction.

7

When I woke for work, four or five inches of snow had fallen, and the grounds were white. I searched a website to confirm that school was closed for the day. C would have the boys, and they would cut out snowflakes, taping them to the living room window. They'd get out the Christmas tree base. When I got home, colored lights would be draped around the room and candles would be lit.

On the way into work, traffic traveled twenty-five miles-per-hour. Spun-out cars waited for State Troopers. One man stood in the snow near the meridian with a cell phone to his ear. Close to the plaza where I worked, a truck had wrapped itself around a telephone pole.

The office was locked and dark when I arrived, so I sat with my back to the door and read *Moby-Dick*, a chapter titled "Ramadan." Queequeg sits for hours in an impenetrable state in a room he shares with Ishmael. Ishmael has already signed up for his berth in the Pequod and has heard that Ahab is an "ungodly, god-like man." After Queequeg comes out of his trance, the two friends take their breakfast and head out to board the ship. They pick their teeth with halibut bones.

JP, the secretary, arrived first. She would only be working in the office another week. She had taken the job to be close to her father, who was dying of lung cancer. She was going to move back South to be with her husband.

JP was too slim by a degree, bird-like, pale. She carried a magazine about yoga with her, and throughout the day she picked at her endless supply of bird-food. The more she ate, the thinner she got. That morning she had granola in a cup mixed with yogurt. JP and I talked until Emily, whose job was to prepare the contracts, arrived. She let us in. As usual, Emily's face was both smile and grimace. She used to be an elementary school teacher.

In the office I checked email. A presenter from Arkansas would let me know next week about a $15,000 contract. I checked the list of people I needed to call. I had to copy their names, their phone numbers and the time of my call. I had to note the nature of our conversation in a grid. On a good day, I would make thirty calls. I'd put a check by each conversation on the grid and highlight it in yellow. Mostly I'd leave voicemail: "Hi, Ken. This is Adam Miller from Richter Artist Management. I wanted to touch base on some information I had sent along, wanted to answer any questions you may have. And, well, we just got some great news in yesterday about the Zephyr Quartet, who've been nominated for a Grammy. We're setting up a tour that will run through Wisconsin in November of '06. Anyway, get back to me when you can. I look forward to talking to you then. Thanks so much. Bye now."

The day sped by. A blur of calls, scribbled notes, letters. At the end of the week, I would compile statistics and check them against my goals, and I would make goals for the next week: conversations, holds, contracts.

"We need to turn holds to gold," I would joke with the director of sales, Ann.

"I love that," she would say. "Turn holds to gold." She copied it down and hung it on a wall in her office.

In the dark of the parking lot, I unlocked the car. Within a minute, it was filled with Beethoven.

8

During the summertime before the year when I graduated, something happened that turned me off from being a professional mortician. There was a fire. I had to pull out four dead children, young kids. That's the day I quit.

> November 29, 1963. I will throw myself insanely back into working. I will exert everything in a mad plunge. I have reached another end. I am in the Stedelijk Museum and am going to have eggs and cheese and milk. Then I am going back to my studio and fight to and with myself to maintain a continuity of work. There must be a result. I must make it. I will force myself into freedom and hope when I get close I can see and know how to be free.

JUST A LIFE

The goal of every musician is to be free, but freedom is rare.

Ahmad Jamal

1

My mother accidentally forwards an email:

> Hi. A quick update on the upper cemetery situation. We've run into a potential snag with allotting space that appears to be open because we may not have all of the outstanding deeds. We're trying to get a better handle on this, but the recordkeeping wasn't very thorough. On May 15th, the Trustees are also going to discuss what our obligation is in terms of honoring deeds indefinitely. That said, there certainly does still appear to be space where trees used to be, we just need to confirm there's nothing in the ground so there are no surprises. This will be done when we do the ground-piercing radar with the state archeologist on June 22nd. I also spoke with Fire Chief Auden yesterday and he confirmed that he does want to sell us back whatever space he has left from his deed. We'll be able to determine exactly where that space is on June 22nd. Chief Auden will join us that morning so, with any luck, we can make him an offer and wrap everything up shortly thereafter. Regards, Dave

2

How're things back in OH? Around here, every birthday takes place at a laser tag facility on an industrial road, which is connected by a network of underground tunnels to places like Magic Mountain (your nickname, Magic Dachau, fits: I remember the blue water spouting from the summit, miniature golf below, the race track, the arcade with broken games, each rectangular room—next to the infernal holding tank of multi-color plastic balls—decked out with pizza, soda, cake, and plastic bin…smoke billowing from the stacks) and the WOW Family Fun Center. The tunnels are populated by flesh eating creatures with glittering eyes. We've been to four of these events with more to follow—each day-glo invitation stuck to the fridge. I drop off one of the boys with a present, pick up two hours later—no hello. Kids emerge from a smoke-filled room and collect a printout with a statistical breakdown of kills. On the way out you grab a party bag with sweets and a present equal to the one you brought: *quid pro quo.*

This past weekend I went to a bar mitzvah back in Bridgeport. My mother squirmed surrounded by Jewish custom. With frustration, she turned the Bible around and around. At the party afterwards (*safely* back in Westport), my aunt—skin puffed and scarred—walked up to me and began to fellate a pig-in-a-blanket. "This little guy's about ready to come," she said and giggled through a grin of rotted teeth. I staggered to my numbered table, where I explained who I was, how I was related. A woman who claimed to know all about my grandmother figured I was, by blood, a Jew. When she heard we were looking for a new house in Columbus, she cited the large Jewish population there: they would go after me. "They're very aggressive, and more and more people are coming back. Especially now." On the dance floor, celebrants lined up for the Electric Slide. I went to get some air and stopped to watch a child dip a strawberry into a waterfall of chocolate next to an immense glass container of blue and white jellybeans. "Did you sign?" a voice asked. On an artist's easel they had mounted a large picture of my cousin's son—he wore a tuxedo and stood with a cello. Guests had signed the image in blue ink.

3

October 12, 1960. The Museum of Modern Art is a strange place. The people are stranger. What are their reasons for looking at these things? They come in droves to sit and talk. It reflects little on their lives. Strange. Strange that Monet's love of light should be viewed without respect. How sad not to know. What are man's real intentions? To express or be trod under. Why not put people in frames? I can't explain. I wish someone could know. But I don't want to cause pain to anyone. Some painters know, and I know. Take my loving wife from me, so she can't feel the pain. My son. My beautiful son. I beg for him not to know, to be content with just a life.

On Chapel Street, plastic bags hung off the sides of the Yale Art Museum. Once inside, a few dollars into a glass container, I spiraled down the nautilus staircase to the modern-design coat hangers. A guard appeared. Five hangers clattered to the ground. The guard nodded.

In the American Colonial section, most of which was closed down, George Washington stood in a portrait taken up by the white expanse of his pants. Except for me, the room was empty, until another guard walked up and said I had to check my briefcase out front. She also said the museum was mostly closed for a year because it had not been renovated for fifty years, and they needed special glass to cut UV rays. The glass was being made in Louisiana, but it had all been flooded. Some modern pieces, maybe the Rothkos I'd come to see, were available now.

Downstairs, around a corner: Van Gogh's painting of a night café on a makeshift wall: gaslights vibrate, the shadow of a pool table darkens. Van Gogh had used the painting as rent. "I have tried," he writes, "to express the terrible passions of humanity by means of red and green." He compares the atmosphere of the café—"a place where one can ruin one's self, run mad or commit a crime"—to a devil's furnace.

Around another corner: torsos, eroded noses. So I retraced my path, entered the museum store and purchased a Rothko biography. A few turned pages: Rothko's suicide—slashed arms and suspicion about his pants, neatly folded on a chair; before that: the aneurysm; earlier in his life: he read Nietzsche's *The Birth of Tragedy.* A museum employee said the Rothko paintings, the ones I had come to see, were in safe storage.

It rained. New Haven was empty like the museum. Back at the parking garage, I rode the cold elevator up to the third floor. Around and around I drove until the bottom, where a guard motioned me to put the car in reverse and go back. *Go back, go back.* Slowly, as I backed towards the first curve, the guard changed his mind. So I pulled up to another guard, handed her three dollars, and the gate lifted.

4

Children slid by on sneakers or chased each other with purple and blue light sabers. Parents with earbuds, laptops. I'd finished a cover letter for a teaching job back in Columbus. Another school cafeteria, another chess tournament. I'd brought a book to read.

My father looked sicker than ever during a recent visit to Westport—pallid skin, thinned hair. He had had a blood transfusion and was recovering from surgery: a metal contraption, implanted, to support eroded bone in his right hand. He called it "The Spider." At lunch when I mentioned that a friend of mine was headed to Vietnam on business, he said he'd been there.

"What?" my mother questioned.

"Don't you remember? I was looking for my son from my first marriage—he was in the service during the war there. Of course, there were a lot of people over there, and I never found him."

On the inside cover of the book, it said that a proportion of the proceeds would go to a worldwide movement to support tribal peoples. Another page in, an epigraph from John Hollow Horn, an Oglala Lakota, 1932: "Some day the earth will weep, she will beg for her life, she will cry with tears of blood. You will make a choice, if you will help her or let her die, and when she dies, you will die."

A girl, purple shirt, light blue pants, knit cap pulled tight to her eyebrows—all the chess players had gone to the tournament room and the shiny floor was hers. She glided and made gestures as though her arms were streamers in a breeze.

CB had told me about times when he could not paint. He called them periods of sterility. He would wait—play golf, work on restoring antiques. Even when being lazy, he had said, he worked on his art. Sooner or later he would stretch canvas.

In Part I of *The Castle*, titled "Arrival," K. observes a dark portrait:

> ...it was indeed a picture, as now became evident, the half-length portrait of a man around fifty. He held his head so low over his chest that one barely saw his eyes, the drooping seemed to be caused by the high, ponderous forehead and the powerful, crooked nose. His beard, pressed in at the chin owing to the position of his head, jutted out farther below. His left hand was spread out in his thick hair but could no longer support his head.

K. wants to know if it is the Count.

When Ishmael enters the Spouter-Inn, he studies a large oil painting, "thoroughly besmoked and every way defaced":

> —It's the Black Sea in a midnight gale.—It's the unnatural combat of the four primal elements.—It's a blasted heath.—It's a Hyperborean winter scene.—It's the breaking-up of the ice-bound stream of Time. But at last all these fancies yielded to that one portentous something in the picture's midst. *That* once found out, and all the rest were plain. But stop; does it not bear a faint resemblance to a gigantic fish? even the great leviathan itself?

At the Inner Station while he waits for transportation to his trading post, Mr. Kurtz paints:

> ...a small sketch in oils, on a panel, representing a woman, draped and blind-folded, carrying a lighted torch. The background was somber—almost black. The movement of the woman was stately, and the effect of the torchlight on the face was sinister.

Early in his book, James Wilson writes down an old, oral account of how white people were created: the hero L'itoi brought victims of a giant killer-eagle back to life—those who had been dead the longest, who were most decayed and pale, became white people. For such a long time these people had been dead, they had forgotten everything, so the hero gave them the power of writing. With written records, they could remember. Wilson concludes that from this "...point of view, literacy is a kind of crutch: far from being an emblem of cultural superiority, it is evidence that Europeans are lost, ignorant and detached from knowledge of themselves."

5

January 20, 1963. Mental problems have become regular for me, and headaches too. At 26 I find it difficult, but I can manage. What is impor-

> tant, right now, is to draw and paint. I feel the aloneness more and more each day, but the drawings are coming along well, and I have finished two paintings. I wrote to Hiler. I want to go see him and work with him again. As I paint and draw, I feel that you must divorce yourself from living to achieve greatness in your work.

A blue sky. Sunday morning, March 19, 2006. CB's journal, which I've stored in a plastic bag, sits on the table next to me. I'd looked at the top page for weeks, each time I took it out, I thought I'd transcribe the journal. The first entry had the time: 4:45PM. Above the time: KULOV VODKA. He's in Dan's Tavern, and he reads a book on philosophy. He is a single man, he writes, and he has just sold a painting. He has received a letter from New York saying he will be arrested in ten days. The word *arrested* is printed in all caps and is spelled like this: ARESSTED. Other words are printed in all caps on that first yellowed page: POWER, BEER, THINKERS, GIFTS. Like Ahmad Jamal, he writes, the POWER is in him, and it is also in the 5 + 10 cent store where he bought the pad of paper.

I cut the pad like a deck of cards and read: he is alone and drunk and going to see Hiler in Paris tomorrow "to see if he can shed any light on the subject." The subject is "this sorry and lonely drunken state" and the need to find a place to live (France or Spain or Italy or Greece), a place where he can be himself. He describes his "self' as selfish and not so clean as he once thought.

In the 1920s Hilaire Hiler owned a club on the Left Bank where he played jazz piano with a live monkey on his back—in 1963, he had three years to live, was an older, established "abstract" artist—a father figure for an aspiring young artist, who, according to CB, will betray him. From another entry: "He [Hiler] is a great man, but also a great old drunk." "Perhaps some day," CB continues, "someone will say the same about me."

Another page, dated June 26, 1963, Dublin, Ireland, he has copied a quote from Homer in caps: "There is nothing stronger and nobler than when a man and wife are of one heart and mind in a house, a grief to their foes, and to their friends great joy, but their own hearts know best." Below that: "For reason more than anything else is man." Aristotle.

On another page, a black ink drawing: a chained skeleton. In its right hand a yo-yo, unwound. In its left, a cord with a plug. The head looks like orbits of electrons.

At the time he's making his journal entries, I'm in my mother's womb in Los Angeles—like the drawing, I have a spine and a cord. I'll be born by Caesarean on December 21, 1963; twenty years later, I'll meet my father for the first time, face to face.

Carefully, I put the cut deck together and store it back in the plastic bag. I packed up and headed into the bright day.

One theory of Rothko's later paintings, the shimmering rectangles, is that they connect to a mass grave: murdered Jews from a czarist pogrom that took place during his youth in Dvinsk. Cossacks had taken the Jewish families from their village out to the woods and commanded them to dig. Imagine a rectangular pit. According to one account, Rothko had been haunted by the vision of the grave; in another, Rothko had witnessed the digging of the grave and the massacre as a child. But in the footnotes of James Breslin's biography, he writes:

> All of the historians I talked with in Daugavpils, as well as the officials with the local Latvian-Jewish Cultural Society, stated unequivocally that there had been no pogroms in Dvinsk, a view supported by Flior's memoir, *Dvinsk*; they also said that they had never heard of mass graves in connection with pogroms, though they would not rule it out as a possibility.

When you perform Samuel Barber's *Adagio for Strings*, you play many flatted notes—even double flats. Such writing for strings darkens and strains the tone of the instruments. And then the moment of unbearable tension, when the conductor implores you to pull as much sound as you can on your instrument, every inch of bow as powerfully as you can, to create one screaming tone in a brutal, sustained shriek. Release. Freeze. The silence that follows, one conductor said, is the most important part of the piece.

Rothko: "Silence is so accurate."

After the silence in Barber's *Adagio*, seven elongated chords—you find the hues of Rothko's rectangles, the dark and diffused acrylics on paper, mounted on canvas or board. Some viewers, encountering Rothko's late paintings for the first time, break down and weep.

6

June 4, 2006. Cars pulled over on Alexander Road, hazard lights blinked. Red and silver glitter slowly fell in the sky above Palmer Stadium. It was the last night of reunions.

The next morning, in front of Nassau Hall, rows of chairs were being aligned and white gates had been set down in front of the Chapel. To the right of the Chapel entrance, a movie screen had been set up and was filled with color bars.

As I worked in Firestone's reference room, I heard a low hum that rose in pitch and volume: mmmmmmm! mmmmmmm! The source, who worked not far from me, spoke loudly at a computer screen: "WE HAVE THIS CONCEPTION BUT WE CANNOT BEAR IT!" Another crescendo hum, and then I heard him say, in a conversational tone, the word "invert."

The two other people in the reference room left, and as one passed by, he smiled and raised his brow. In a more subdued voice, I heard the word "settings."

A couple walked in and the woman pointed at the man. They left. I waited. The man stood, hummed a swoop and a swish, and turned so I could see the picture on his t-shirt: a broiling ball of gas, solar flares, eruptions, turbulence, flames. His hair was a halo-mass of Brillo. He walked over to a shelf of books without picking one, then turned and walked back to the computer. For the next half hour he was quiet.

Through the library windows I saw families gathering—action without sound: a man wore an orange hat and embraced another man. A father gave his daughter a ride on his shoulders. Clouds were thick and gray.

> September 10, 1963. I would rather paint in an institution. Think of going insane. Instead of ending with death you begin with insanity. You escape with your mind, so you also escape your body. I could write a book on going insane in one easy lesson. But can you get out and write or paint if you were all the way out? Who would care? Would you care? I wonder if all people think insanity is a weakness. Or if people even think. First, be a hermit, alone. No one to talk, no one to misunderstand, not even a doctor. I wonder if you know it's coming or if it just happens. Maybe you can block out the faces. And not hear.

7

October 4, 2006. The Buckeyes were undefeated: certain of purpose, well conditioned. Anticipation was high. A life insurance company ran ads on billboards along High Street that referenced defeated opponents (slashed out) and the weekend's upcoming victim. The tag line: LIFE COMES AT YOU FAST.

While I waited to pick up Aidan in the line of private school SUVs, I listened to a radio interview of a reporter who had been embedded with troops in Iraq. His hand had been blown off. What did he think when he first looked down to see a stump, asked the interviewer. The reporter had just published a book about his experience, and as he talked about his decision to use a stainless steel hook instead of the high-tech hand, I pulled the car up a few more feet to a speed bump.

Later, the day's events revised their own narratives on my computer: a professional football player's attempted suicide; no, he had not attempted suicide; a man walked into a school and killed students; a man walked into a school with the intent of sexually molesting girls, then called his wife, then killed students then killed himself; here was the man's journal with the list of what he needed for the task; the man was haunted by the past; the man had molested family members in the past; the man had dreams of what he would do; the man was angry at God; the community was close and would bring meals for weeks to the families who lost children, and they would share the burden of grief.

Chatwin thinks he is going blind. He constantly squints and the world is a blur. Chatwin's blindness is Oedipal in nature, if not in deed. With hysteria he casts out the offending eye, no longer able to look upon what his life has become. Sotheby's, where he had worked and risen on a fast track, is a place where "...you felt like you were working for a rather superior kind of funeral parlor." In a move that heals psychic wounds, he casts himself out and travels to the Sudan.

Chatwin arrives in Khartoum on February 5, 1965. He will go on an expedition to the Red Sea Hills to look for kaolin deposits, ride on camels toward the Rift Valley, ride through the Valley of Shadows. He will change his life.

I looked up from the biography to see a man holding a cell phone into the air. He aimed northwest at the cloudy morning sky to photograph a rainbow.

Just the night before I had told Eli about refracted light. We talked about our sun and the next star and how far away it was and how long it would take to get there. Eli was seven.

I kneeled down next to the refrigerator. Isaiah wanted a hug before school. I held his little body up to mine. I ran my hand through his fiery hair.

In Social Studies, Aidan's sixth-grade class arrived at the six pages about the Israelites. We studied together for his quiz. When I told him he was related by blood to this history, he pounded his chest once with his fist then waved outward making a peace sign. I helped him memorize the titles of the five books: Genesis, Exodus,

Leviticus, Numbers, Deuteronomy. Saul before David. Define *diaspora*. What did Moses call Canaan? Six hundred years in Egypt.

Aidan told me, yeah, they had seen a movie, and he imitated the voice and manner of Moses parting the waters. His quiz will have ten multiple-choice questions. Pesky Romans and Hebrew National Hotdogs. He'll miss two questions on the quiz, move on to the next ancient civilization to be quizzed, and go to the football game on Saturday. I'll cart him to a birthday party that night at a bowling alley, and park near a mud splattered truck fitted with a row of high-powered searchlights that flies both the American flag and the Confederate flag off its flat-bed.

For the stars of heaven and the constellations thereof shall not give their light: the sun shall be darkened in his going forth, and the moon shall not cause her light to shine.

8

Jogging. Sunoco stickers on street signs. A sign on a post: CAMELOT: COTTAGES TO CASTLES. Plots had been cleared. Burr Farms Elementary School, where I had spent grades 1-6, razed years ago, now mini-mansions with farm motif—a decorative silo built into the side of each house. But I stopped on a spot that used to be black-top for kickball and four-square, where Frank Fiorello used to pound left-footed homeruns over the right-field fence into the swing set, jungle gym, sandbox, where I sat alone, first grade, mesmerized by tornado swirls of sand and leaves. Frank, although short, was the best athlete in our grade and had won a local contest: Punt, Pass, and Kick. This gave him a power I wanted. And although I got in a lot of fights in elementary school during recess, I did not want to fight Frank. He was preternaturally strong, and I preferred him as a friend, even though after a visit to his house, it became clear that friendship would not take. Once, during a P.E. demonstration for parents, Frank was positioned standing in front of a raised pommel horse, and I vaulted over him—I remember his smile as I ran towards him, and how he crossed his hands over his crotch.

Frank has been dead for many years, a car crash into a tree that also took the life of Grant Peterson, whom we called Granny and who had snuck a beer onto the bus on the way to a middle school basketball game. I was told Frank's father visited his son's grave regularly, and that the grief caused his own death. Frank's father had taken him out of public school, sent him to a private school where he thought he would have better athletic opportunities.

I cut through the line of pine trees that had been the school boundary, jogged to the high school with its multi-million dollar facelift so that it resembled all suburban schools: curve of brick and tinted glass. Jogged around back to the fields, empty, angled down the hill to the diamond. Walked down the first base path toward home, stood in the batter's box and felt the distance to the fence.

The track was rubber, no longer cinder. The football field, the synthetic grass, the letters, lines, in white and blue and yellow, impossibly sharp to the eye—a digital world: no dirt, no hiss, no pop. Up the hill, the parking lot, 007 painted white on the windows of student cars with slogans for the upcoming game.

Two emergency vehicles were parked in front of the school. I passed the security car positioned in the center of the main entrance, waved to the man keeping watch, and he waved back. Took a right and then a left onto Terhune, where another Sunoco sticker had been stuck on the sign, toward Teddy Friedman's house.

On Terhune, many of the lots and houses were the same, more overgrown with worn paint jobs, the people who were new forty years ago, like my parents, hanging on. One new mini-mansion hulked up close to the small street. The house was as bright as a magazine cover, a circular trampoline netted in.

I climbed the outcropping of rock and walked to a thicket where Teddy and I had hidden with a Styrofoam cup full of lawn mower gasoline. When he lit the gas, we watched the flame stay contained, just as he said it would, until I panicked and stomped on it. The flames leaped into the dry summer leaves, raced up the trees.

Suburban danger of the past—the golf-pro's son burned down the house, killed his two brothers; a man fell asleep at the wheel one morning and plowed into children at a bus stop knocking one child dead up into the branches of a tree. One boy, a member of our church and a boy scout, had hanged himself in the family's garage.

We ran, rang a neighbor's doorbell, ran into Teddy's garage and filled a pail with water, and when we returned: flames to the sky and sirens in the distance. A pail's worth of water was tossed into the conflagration that looked like a stray napalm strike from the war on TV.

I jogged through Teddy's backyard and saw an addition to the house. All evidence of the pool had been smoothed away with lawn—we had swum in that pool until our eyes throbbed. Then we would go, barefoot with wet suits into the house. It was freezing and strange: newly installed central air and shag rug. Teddy's father was the reigning pediatrician in Westport, and worked in a complex of doctor's offices called Fort Apache. Dr. Friedman was a hunter when on vacation, and in the den lay a bear rug, head intact, the jaws frozen open to reveal teeth and a stiff pink tongue.

The man mowing the lawn saw a forty-two-year-old white man in sweatpants and sweatshirt loping through pachysandra and shadow, stumbling on the old stones that had been used to separate plots of land. The hired hand wore headphones and steered the mower away. In the distance the home of a little league coach who had hanged himself like the boy from church. My best friend's mother, an EMT on call that day, had helped take him down.

The loop was almost complete, and to my right I saw the finished castles of Westport—no drawbridge, no moat, no dragon, no damsel in distress—just lots of rooms with a gazebo attached and primary colored play structures big enough for a school's playground on the front lawn.

I stopped at a small pond. Its borders were now so overgrown that it was hidden from the street.

At recess the pond was off-limits. Now I stood and looked into the water and watched it trickle, as it had back then, from the pond through the concrete tunnel that lead beneath the street to the other side. Climbing into the tunnel, we had grabbed tadpoles as they flapped in the stream. Then we stuck them full of thorns, and tossed them on the street where we'd see them days later mashed into the pavement.

The colors of the leaves ran red and yellow. The woods filled with counter-caw, low and high, of crow and blue jay, creak of catbird, warble of morning dove, the electronic DEE—DEE—DEE of chickadee. A dense chirp, a molten triangle of sound: a cardinal.

The songbirds, which welcomed me home when nothing else did, I had hunted with perfect eye and BB gun and collected in a paint can like a serial killer at the base of the weeping willow outside our garage. Their vivid colors and markings, their musical DNA, I had internalized while tracking and killing. The blackest grackle crackled like blown circuitry with twelve others in our front yard's birch tree. When held close: the feathers seemed as though they had been painted with a mixture of oil and gasoline: rainbows radiated from the blackness.

My elementary school had been situated between its namesake, Burr's farm, and Rippe's farm. We raided Rippe's strawberry patches near the end of each school year, and he'd chase us out brandishing a shotgun, the shells stuffed with salt. Then he hired someone to chase us—we assumed him to be a track star from the high school. Whoever he was, we saw him break from the barn, and off we went. From a thick branch on the tree across from the cafeteria, heart racing, I looked down to see the top of Bobby Paulson's head—he was a redheaded, overweight boy. He was being dragged to the principal's office.

Rippe's strawberries: we'd run them into the woods to a trickling stream that fed the pond, rinse them, and each bite had dirt, sweetness, and warmth from having just been pulled from sun-stroked patches.

But nothing remains except the hidden pond. That makeshift school, propped up to house and educate the growing population of the 1950s, had not been built to last. Burr Farms Elementary School: Mr. Petrillo, third grade, with hairy forearms. He had played Triple A ball my mother said. That explained the arms. He sold encyclopedias in the summer, door-to-door, and came to our house one day. Mr. Petrillo told me I needed to stop causing fights. So I did. Mr. Alverson, fourth grade, who puffed cherry tobacco from his pipe and kept a rattlesnake head suspended in a jar of formaldehyde—for him, I memorized every part of the digestive system, every part of the ear and the eye, outer and inner.

Then there was Mrs. Connors, who made me play "Turkey in the Straw" on the violin in front of the school, made me miss recess to rehearse, and thought I was a musical boy. Mrs. Connors was old, powdered her face, and she could be mean. Once I had peeked through the small rectangular window of her heavy classroom door and watched as she removed the gray ball of hair from her head and dropped it, still criss-crossed with needles, into a desk drawer.

For years around Halloween, she had told us about the movie we weren't old enough to see yet, a movie in which we would see the dead rise from the grave. "But not yet, you're too young." I expected images of concentration camps: that was a place where they tortured men by inserting glass tubes into their penises, then brought in a beautiful woman, the effect of which was followed by the smashing of the tube. I didn't want to see that. But the movie, called *Night on Bald Mountain*, was just a filmstrip, the kind that beeped, with images from paintings. We groaned.

We had waited for years for this moment, this indoctrination into the forbidden. Mrs. Connors turned off the lights and started the record hissing and popping. Violins: quietly and quickly. Mrs. Connors swayed with the music. Suddenly, she thrust her face near to mine, her wrinkled cheeks filled with air like a human blowfish, and violently exhaled. The music grew louder. A choir of trombones sang harsh tones of gold and brown, and Mrs. Connors swooped up and down the aisles, arms stretched out, screeching: "I'm a banshee! I'm a banshee!"

The music swirled in my head as I concentrated on the screen: *dark towers, windows lit with flame, beams of white light and billowing clouds of smoke; devils walking catwalks and climbing ladders; armies with banners of black, red, white, charging the barren countryside; bodies climbing out of a fire-reflecting lake; a man dragged to the scaffold; another man bent over, legs the trunks of trees rooted in two wooden boats, body an egg, buttocks cracked to reveal a woman in an apron tapping wine from a jug; a bored man leaning on a cracked shell; a reluctant man, naked, led by the hand by a long-billed bird.*

I passed houses where workers mowed lawns and bagged leaves and took a right onto Long Lots Road. I knew these sidewalks well. From earlier in my run, I had known exactly where the paved path humped from the roots of an old tree, ridged and cracked next to an 18th-century house with its identification plaque, right by a bend in North Avenue where a white toy poodle had been struck by a car and lay dead on a spring day. We had pulled over on our way home from school to see what could be done. An apostrophe of red had pooled next to it on the newly paved street.

On the seventh floor of Saint Vincent's, my father's room smelled like piss. When I walked over to the window, each step peeled. Bridgeport spread out below, and I saw children leaving Read Elementary School. Propped up in the hospital bed, my father: a mound above his left eye; body wasted; a bulge in his upper chest looked like a doorknob shrink-wrapped in skin. He called the nurse. Too late. But he wore diapers, and he called them diapers.

My mother arrived the next day. She had a tube that came out of her shirt and fed into a plastic container she had wedged into her pocketbook: it filled with drips of blood. I took notes about dosages.

The next morning, all of us home, I was on my knees and worked socks onto swollen feet, then shoes. I tied my father's shoelaces.

When my mother left the house to buy a mask for his nebulizer, I took a shower, and when I got out, I heard my father heading down steps to the basement.

"Where are you going?"

"I need to find something."

"The last thing you should be doing is going down the stairs."

But he had his will. He also had a 9MM handgun in his drawer of his nightstand. Next to the nightstand he had hung pictures of wolves in snowy woods.

I looked out the kitchen window: he was on his knees, and the upper half of his body was inside the car.

Into my head Bach's *Suite Number 5 in E minor*, as I rode the Connecticut Limo to LaGuardia. We stopped down in Stamford to pick-up other passengers. Piles of dirt and stone, new buildings. Sun: bright. Blue sky. The clouds looked like photographic negatives of flak. When I had driven to the hospital on the day I had arrived, the clouds had been spread like wet sand across the horizon.

My father's shins flaked, and his feet were light purple. At the base of his spine, it looked as if a metal rod had been inserted. The doctors wanted to do a spinal tap to examine the disfiguration of a chromosome in his blood.

My mother panicked when she could not find the limo pick-up stop. She ran a red light, drove in circles. The blood in her plastic container looked like strawberry Kool-Aid.

The limo, which was a charter bus, pulled onto I-95 South. A sign read STAMFORD DOWNTOWN DAY AND NIGHT THE ARTS.COM. Concrete, glass, geometry. A pyramid mass of dirt covered with a blue tarp. From the bridge before Cos Cob, I saw Long Island Sound shimmering with sunlight. The trees, close and far, were in an early stage of ignition.

After my mother's surgery, she was elated. Her parents, my dead grandparents, she said, had been in the room with her.

WELCOME TO NEW YORK with a picture of the Statue of Liberty. Stone on each side of the interstate was scarred with vertical lines, drill holes down which dynamite had been dropped and exploded to clear the path for interstate pavement. For many other miles: sound barrier walls made to look like wood. We caught up to a train that rode on tracks parallel to the highway. TRUMP PLAZA CONDOS were underway with a five-story banner of Trump's face fastened to scaffolding. Home Depot, Linens and Things, Co-op City, slag heaps, and the Golden Arches a thousand feet in the air. Remnants of marshland. SUCCUMB TO SMOOTH alliterated in a beer ad.

We headed to the George Washington Bridge and passed pet shops, law offices, FOOD, lower rates, free consultations. A graveyard: line after line of stone cropped close like a cornfield. Saint Joseph's School for the Deaf. A large cross with words engraved: I WILL COME BACK.

Towards the Bronx-Whitestone Bridge, which angled like a launch pad, the bus increased speed, clouds sped like in a time-elapse film, the surrounding water for miles, wind-beaten, turned to liquid mercury. New York City, with its skyscrapers and Empire State Building, flickered like sparks thrown into air.

9

My biological father writes in his journal about a power, and he uses caps when he writes about it. He personifies it, says he will take the power with him to a party. It is a sin to the power, the power is in him, the power exists, Hiler has the POWER+. He wonders if he is capable of possessing the power. He gives his life freely to it. The power demands things. To deny this is to be hypocritical. Once one has the power, there is no life for the body. Realize the power, life leaves. If he were in Cuba, where he had been stationed for a time during the Korean War, *the hours would be honest and have POWER.* The power has true rhythm. The power draws all breath. Such knowledge, he writes, makes it difficult to exist in society. He lives not as himself, but as a tool to the power. He lives between two worlds. He is a parasite on this world, but his parasitism is justified because it feeds creativity. He is offered $200 for a large green painting. He considers spending the summer in the mountains. *Good-bye old world.* He drinks CC. He is high. He worries about losing his government allowance and VA benefits. He hopes to hear something from the University of New Mexico. *No news of my son. POWER is upon this, but it's cold and BLACK.*

10

February 28, 1961. In a coffee house. Not a soul here. I have my props: a candle in a glass and ashtray and a mug of beer. So I sit alone and write. It reminds me of Dan's Tavern in Old New Jersey. The reflection of candlelight makes an interesting problem. The table has a dark stain, the top of the glass is transparent, the candle is yellow-white, the beer is the color of the tabletop with a white and brandy color froth. The pad is black with white pages. The cigarette smoke, the texture of the ashes, and a burnt match in the smooth ashtray. A white china dish with two quarters in it. It is a warm brandy color because of the dark beer and the candlelight.

The OSU basketball team lost the national championship, just like the football team. The headline of the Columbus Dispatch: **TWICE BITTEN**. The merchandise at Starbucks has turned to bunnies in polka-dot bowls with chocolate eggs. A lime green tablecloth is draped over a larger black one that decorates two circular display tables. On one, a sign read: *GIVING IS RECEIVING.* On the other, pictures of three artists with the sentence *I AM STARBUCKS.* One artist is from Costa Rica, has been painting for forty years and finds inspiration for her work in color and all things related to nature. Her goal, the tag continues, is to communicate joy and positive energy. That goal is realized in the lovely ceramic mug you can buy: *Made in China. 2006 Starbucks Coffee Company. All rights reserved.* Then I grab something called Lemon Paper. One of the other pictured artists created the design, and she is passionate about honesty, humility and tolerance. "Yami" strives to express the free spirit and exotic essence of Costa Rica in her art, as well as the harmonious relationship between her work and the environment. Did you know Chinese rulers engaged in wars of gift giving, trying to outdo each other with spectacular presents? *GIVING IS GRATITUDE; I GIVE BACK.*

A VISUAL SATISFACTION

In Xanadu did Kubla Kahn
A stately pleasure-dome decree:
Where Alph, the sacred river, ran
Through caverns measureless to man
Down to a sunless sea.

"Kubla Khan or, a Vision in a Dream": A Fragment.
Samuel Taylor Coleridge

1

Finally, I managed to be, at a party, riding a little red wagon with her while someone pulled us along. It was first grade. I was madly in love. We hit a bump, and I used the bump as a subterfuge and went over and kissed her. She got very upset. I aimed for her mouth but hit her ear.

While I transcribed audiotape, parents and children walked by on their way to school. Signs were mounted on a lamppost: white trumpets pointed skyward.

My father clears his throat. He coughs. He calls to my mother: *Margot!* She yells back from upstairs.

We had recorded in his office—a dilapidated studio-apartment in our backyard where he used to stay up all night writing ad copy for American Express, or a chair that would spring the elderly to their feet, or the miracle of aloe, or vaginal itch cream. I'd push the button on the intercom system to call him to dinner.

The office on that summer day in 2002 smelled like mildew and rot. Mice had left droppings on the couch in front of his desk. Spider web and mummified insects were stuck in the skylight. Buzzing and tapping. An ad for Lucky Strike, in yellowed newsprint, framed on a wall: my father's twenty-five-year-old head floats in a red circle. He smiles. A cigarette juts from an open pack.

> There was a pause of profound stillness, then a match flared, and Marlow's lean face appeared, worn, hollow, with downward folds and dropped eyelids, with an aspect of concentrated attention.
> (Joseph Conrad, *Heart of Darkness*)

The D.A.T. recorder catches every sound. Thunder peals above. My father lights up.

When I was a little boy, he had shown me the trap door beneath his feet where he sat at his desk. He propped it open. I peered into the foundation. The walls were made of dirt. He told me that the space had been used to hide escaped prisoners and slaves.

Nightly, I could not escape the seductive ritual of placing myself in the pit: train tracks, chains, and human bones glowed in the darkness. It was cool and damp and overrun with spiders. When the flashlight gave out, my yells unheard, I clawed into the walls. Dirt lodged in my fingernails. It was a slow suffocation. The intensity of the visualization, the sweat-inducing power of it, was rivaled only by another: the vision of Hannah Gross, my first grade crush. She stood in my bedroom doorway. She wore white.

2

On September 3, 1882, Van Gogh writes to his brother Theo:

> Yesterday evening I was working on a slightly rising woodland slope covered with dry, mouldering beech leaves. The ground was light and dark reddish-brown, emphasized by the weaker and stronger shadows of trees casting half-obliterated stripes across it. The problem, and I found it a very difficult one, was to get the depth of colour, the enormous power & solidity of that ground—and yet it was only while I was painting it that I noticed how much light there was still in the dusk—to retain the light as well as the glow, the depth of that rich colour, for there is no carpet imaginable as splendid as that deep brownish-red in the glow of an autumn evening sun, however toned down by the trees.

3

September 17, 1963. With enthusiasm I went to the New Church here in Amsterdam and tried to paint, from 1PM-5PM, the feeling I had. The problem was the feeling came from the mass feeling of this church. It took a century to build. I am no one. I am nothing. They are rebuilding the church and have been working on it for 5 years and expect it to take at least 15 more to complete. The conclusion: it takes time to make something last. To make something of value. Today I go back to draw. Same day, 2:30PM: the drawing did not go well. The perspective inside the church is difficult. I will wait and go back. I need something on perspective to help me. I need it for this kind of job.

4

October 8, 1961. Can I say a few words about this beautiful sunrise? Kenton plays in the background. I am in a little coffee shop overlooking the entire bay and ocean. The sun is coming up on the other side. The sky is a gas of color, warm air, and a soft breeze. Small buildings are in silhouette against the sky. Music picks up and I pick up on fast moving cars on the highway and more strength in the breeze. The bamboo bush is being moved now. Everything is alive, and so am I.

5

The US grenades, unlike anyone else's, were just little hand-held things, about two pounds, and they were serrated, so that when they exploded, it broke off in pieces about the size of my thumbnail. It would do, hopefully, severe injury to anyone at whom you had thrown it.

6

Artists and mystics have long criticized the modern medicalization of hallucinations, portraying the process as a secularizing attempt to pathologize religious or spiritual experience. Certainly popular attitudes to hallucination have been transformed across the last thousand years. In the Platonic tradition of classical philosophy, the subjective vision was celebrated as a form of privileged insight beyond the phenomenal experience of the external world. Likewise in the Christian and Jewish religions the objective quality of the inner hallucination had long been regarded as a proof of its spiritual reality, although its origin could have been either demonic or divine. (*Oxford Medical Dictionary*)

7

Sunday, September 16, 2007. After having moved to St. Louis, I flew back to Columbus for a convention. In the room on the 14th floor of the hotel, I pulled back the curtains. A spider hung within the double-plated glass. Behind the spider, cars traveled east and west on the interstate or circled the interchanges.

During the day, I met with presenters—the directors of performing arts centers across the Midwest. They flocked into the convention room, a space that also served as a sports venue: dormant scoreboards were mounted above our heads. The presenters wore pink colored ID badges. Exhibitors wore blue. Heads nodded down, raised up.

To my right was an agent who represented an animal trainer. The trainer showed up wearing a safari outfit and deeply tanned skin. To my left, Broadway shows and two young women, one who wore a girlish dress and cowboy boots. Straight ahead: a life-size photo of a magician crouched in a box.

Lunch was in a ballroom. For entertainment, an a cappella group from London did musical shtick. For their encore they imitated an old record player: music modulated in blurs of pitch. The disc slowed, sped. Hiccup repeats. The needle stuck in a groove. Hiss, pops, and skips. The arm slid to the center of the record: *FFFFFFFFFFFF.* Applause. The sound system whined.

The keynote speaker referred to her Minnesotan accent, told stories about her father and how they interpreted the world differently: the generation gap. She had written a book based on *tons* of research that would help presenters develop strategies to appeal to the younger generation of concertgoers. How to get their butts in seats. The twenty to forty age group, you see, need multi-sense stimulation. They want a user-friendly environment. Guess what really improves their experience: nobody wants to touch door handles. *Who knew?* As she spoke, two large screens reinforced what she said with synchronized words and images. The speaker had short hair, a suit, and she wore a headset. She was vigorous, and like a well-traveled stand-up comic, she had timing.

In an elevator, one man said to another, "I'll tell you one thing—there is no chance I'll sell him semen again." They wore jeans and belts with large buckles. I looked down at my gray suit and the badge that hung from my neck.

In the morning, I yanked back the curtains: the spider, and behind it, the sun rose.

8

A private collection of Rothkos can be viewed in St. Louis if you show up at the right time on the right day.

9

My new home office faced north and got sunlight all day. The walls were yellow. Mahogany statues, which my father brought back from the Philippines, stood on the rug. One was male. One was female. Long earlobes bore the weight of earrings. Bones had been thrust through nostrils. Their elongated faces had been carved out of tree trunks. They were, and continue to be, serene and imperturbable. Watercolors painted by my biological father, and the lithograph of a moonlit ocean he had restored just before he died, leaned up against walls.

I flew back to Westport for my father's interment ceremony. The night before, in bed, C had said, "You know, it's just ashes."

After she had fallen asleep and already had begun to dream, I woke her. I didn't think they were just ashes. She said, "Of course, there is something more symbolic about them."

We went to sleep.

My mother wanted my brother and me to lower the small box into the ground. Nightly, she rehearsed the words she wanted to say over the grave.

At the funeral, the honor guard fired rifles outside the church in the parking lot, out of our sight. That day, it had been a mock interment ceremony. A cemetery plot had not been secured.

The report of the weapons was a surprise, and my cousin's daughter sobbed. We had gathered in an open-air courtyard inside the church in the columbarium. For a certain price, your ashes could be stored in a kind of mail slot with a plaque. No one had liked that option for my father. As we stood, I recognized engraved names.

In slow motion steps, as he stared at a fixed point in the distance, a marine carried a flag. Step by step, he made it to my mother. He handed her the flag. He saluted. She said, *Semper Fi.* The marine left as slowly as he had arrived.

Roses were distributed. We walked forward and dropped the flowers on the box. I held Isaiah's hand and helped him place his rose so it would not fall off the box. My mother was last. Her rose, unlike all the others, was white. In the Far East, she later explained, white symbolizes death.

10

After a severe breakdown, Kafka retreats to a mountain village. It is January, 1922. The first evening, he writes in his diary: "The strange, mysterious, perhaps dangerous, perhaps redeeming consolation of writing." In that mountain village, Kafka starts to write *The Castle*:

> It was late evening when K. arrived. The village lay under deep snow. There was no sign of the Castle hill, fog and darkness surrounded it, not even the faintest gleam of light suggested that large Castle. K. stood a long time on the wooden bridge that leads from the main road to the village, gazing upward into the seeming emptiness.

11

A call to attention. You lift your head from the notes you had been reading. You fumble with the program. The score calls for tuba and trombones to descend in steps that grow in brutality. When they arrive at the bottom, trumpets blare, louder, the same call. A force gathers: a punch. A second punch. Pain lifts your body. You are dragged, arms extended from sides. A force drives you skyward and earthward. You are free. You float in the air above the proscenium. Sixty seconds of music has elapsed. For the composer, Piotr Ilych Tchaikovsky, the music is programmatic: Fate holds a sword above a head and prepares to slash down.

12

Nietzsche writes that the Dionysian artist identifies himself with the primal unity, its pain and contradiction. Then:

> Assuming that music has been correctly termed a repetition and a recast of the world, we may say that he [the Dionysian artist or lyrist] produces the copy of this primal unity as music. Now, however, under the Apollonian dream inspiration, this music reveals itself to him again as a *symbolic dream image.* The inchoate, intangible reflection of the primordial pain in music, with its redemption in mere appearance, now produces a second mirroring as a specific symbol...the "I" of the lyrist therefore sounds from the depth of his being. (Friedrich Nietzsche, *The Birth of Tragedy*)

13

Your dead student stands on the corner of High Street and Lane Avenue. A devil's face—the type carved into a mask, a demon from the *Tibetan Book of the Dead*—grimaces in the canopy of leaves outside your child's second-story window. Decapitated and writhing, a snake-haired head hovers in the palm of your hand while you stand in a bathroom. A blast of trumpet knocks you off a couch. Whales dive and surface in pavement as you walk alone at 3AM. It is what you've done with a knife to your left forearm on a counter-top.

Go see a psychiatrist. He'll say, "You must cast out the *demons.*" When he sees your reaction, and you say you are not Christian, he changes to cognitive-behavioral therapy. Plug in positive images to replace negative ones.

"You seem like a person with good impulse control." That's what he says when you say you feel unsafe around your own child, when you describe images.

"Would you like drugs to help?"

"No."

"Then I see you want a natural delivery."

He defines post-traumatic stress disorder. Suicidal ideation.

Then you rise on a swelling tide of mania: "To me it has to do with circles, the big circle and the little circle, or maybe there are hundreds of circles, who knows? But most people can get by when the little circle comes to its low point, or its insane point. It is harder with the big circle. That was 1985, and I did take drugs. The psychiatrist who prescribed the pills had survived a concentration camp. So had his wife. He was short, Jewish, old, reminded me of my grandfather. Anyway, I liked him, too, because he told me a truth. He said, 'I can't help you.' Numbers vibrated on his arm. It was winter and snow had fallen. I lived inside a cork. The outside world was oblivion. White. Fragments from Mozart's *Requiem* played without stop, in loops, in my head. The soprano's voice was an ice-axe. My body was numb. In an old, Victorian style house in Maine, I grabbed a hot radiator to see if I could feel. Dials in a dashboard glowed orange as I drove through mountains curtained in black. I was in a room. A violin played through a speaker. The room tilted forty-five degrees. At the kitchen table, I heard my father say, *Sufficient unto the day is the evil thereof.* At night I sweated in a fetal position. I held my penis. The room spun. I dreamt. My mother swung from the ceiling, upside down. Her lips were black. My head was wedged into a conch shell. I slid down, around and around, snug within a block of ice. In the mornings, the sheets were soaked, and I mistook them for an ocean. In January, I stopped the pills. Not all pills, though. I needed to stop the other pain. I read William Blake. The depression lifted. Years later I met a violinist of a string quartet, an alcoholic, who had a son with my name. The violinist read Camus at night, and he could play the passages of a late Beethoven quartet like an angel—did you know about Beethoven's suicide letters? Composers, painters, poets. Tchaikovsky tried to drown himself. The violinist told me a story about a connoisseur of chamber music who, although he could not play an instrument himself, had a perfect understanding of music. The man demonstrated. He put a record on a turntable. Then he started to form circles in the air with his hands. The circles rotated fast or slow, grew big or small. Each circle was connected mathematically to the music as it played. Music of the spheres. But, you see, when the big circle and the little circle line up at their lowest points: Van Gogh stands in the wheat field. Crows are startled into flight."

The psychiatrist says he is intrigued by the theory of circles and has written it down in his notes. Above his head, three crosses float in a murky picture of stained glass.

14

In July of 1890, Vincent van Gogh returns to Auvers. He writes to his brother and sister-in-law.

> So—having arrived back here, I have set to work again—although the brush is nearly falling from my hands—and because I knew exactly what I wanted to do, I have painted three more large canvases. They are vast stretches of wheat under troubled skies, and I didn't have to put myself out very much in order to try and express sadness and extreme loneliness.

Van Gogh's coffin was covered with yellow flowers. The painter Bernard said that yellow was his favorite color, "a symbol of the light of which he dreamed both in his heart and in his work."

15

November 12, 2007

This morning: Bach's *contrapuncti* with Gould at the helm. So the *Art of the Fugue* is the blueprint for the creation of the world. Each thing you see, the curves of a woman's body, a little girl with ponytails and pink jacket, the copper leaves in the park—Bill, what I'm saying is that we are the other voices suggested, hinted at, transposed, modulated, inverted, backwards played, you name it, and that Bach intuited the order of the universe and used the human rules of musical composition, which is what a genius does: counterpoint—the explosion of many ideas simultaneously, my boy. Big Bang, indeed—the scientists just don't know the right bang to study. The friction between rules and given form and the improvisatory spirit (which is sexual in nature) gives us this life. Few people grasp both—they might get good at one. Jazz is the answer if the right person asks the right question. A great artist senses it—eyes, ears, mouth, nose, touch. Remember those Japanese firebombs we ate—the orange color. Were some of them pink? Think of the presentation! Yes, you have to hold it in your mouth as long as possible, and then: BAP! Tears well in our eyes. Now I also know that one's pain can lead to a communion with the above, or to self-annihilation. This knowledge is secret, complicated, and dangerous. What is exhausting is the re-evaluation of one's values. I'm in that now. The world I created is inverted: it is under the ocean time. Ahoy, Captain! My lungs are strong, but I can barely lift my arms. Of course, all this proposed understanding means shit without the creation of art that allows for sympathetic vibration. In the Kill-The-Lesser-Artist Game (and Copeland, alas, never existed still) the pleasure is in the recognition of how central each of these humans is for us to breathe another breath. It is like the little boy's game of imagining his father dead—attending that funeral. Brother Bill—that was not a game for you. You wore your dead father's checkered shirt until it was in tatters. And while I imagined my father dead when I was a child (only to affirm and to take pleasure in just how powerful he was to me and my imagination), I couldn't imagine my biological father dead because he was already a ghost. So you want to listen to a *contrapunctus*? The worm, he licks my bone. Follow that musical idea to its logical conclusion and I'll see you on the other side—it is all one piece—full of sound and fury, signifying that I am your friend, the idiot, AKA: The Man Who Sold The World.

16

A white steeple set in a blue sky.

This prototypical New England church had been burned down by the British and rebuilt. Silver cups, fashioned by Paul Revere, were safely kept within. We attended most Sundays and never missed the Easter service or the Candlelight Ceremony Christmas Eve.

For me, Christianity never took. I was confirmed only to not upset my parents and attended the confirmation retreat under duress. The highlight of that rainy weekend, which was spent cabin-bound in the Connecticut woods, centered on a magazine that Tim Dickens had smuggled in. It featured a man who could tie his penis in a knot.

When the war in Vietnam was proclaimed over, we all headed to the church to ring the bell. In the balcony in the back of the church, a straw colored rope, about two thirds of an inch in thickness and soft to the touch, hung down through a small hole in the white ceiling.

> Of late years the Manilla rope has in the American fishery almost entirely superseded hemp as a material for whale-liners; for, though not so durable as hemp, it is stronger, and far more soft and elastic; and I will add (since there is an aesthetics in all things), is much more handsome and becoming to the boat, than hemp. Hemp is a dusky, dark fellow, a sort of Indian; but Manilla is as a golden-haired Circassian to behold. (Herman Melville, *Moby-Dick*)

My father rang the hell out of the bell (people remarked on this and it filled me with pride). The act of sounding the bell required not just strength, but a sense of rhythm and timing. The moment to apply force was key. I was allowed to try.

When the rope came down from the ceiling, I was supposed to grab it and pull down. Because I wanted to show off a strength at least similar to my father's and therefore superior to the other boys who would be given a turn, I didn't hear all of the instructions. I was too focused on the task.

Quickly, the rope snaked down from above my head. I jumped up (part of my plan), grabbed on and pulled down as hard as my nine-year-old body would allow. When I got to the carpeted floor, I heard a weak clang, and then the rope pulled back so fast and with such force that, reflexively, I held on. Before I could comprehend—people shouted to let go, LET GO! I was hoisted, bodily, towards the hole above, but my stomach told a different story: I was upside down and falling into the whiteness below.

> But not yet have we solved the incantation of this whiteness, and learned why it appeals with such power to the soul; and more strange and far

> more portentous—why, as we have seen, it is at once the most meaning symbol of spiritual things, nay, the very veil of the Christian Deity; and yet should be as it is, the intensifying agent in things the most appalling to mankind. (Herman Melville, *Moby-Dick*)

The weight of my body slowed the rope. My father had grabbed me. I let go. The bell did not sound. My legs shook and my body felt like jelly. I didn't know which way was up. On the way down the winding stairwell, I gripped the railing.

We walked from the church's parking lot into the old graveyard to its back edge where a small site had been prepared beneath pine trees. The ground was uneven, and I had to steady my aunt as we walked around stones. My uncle, who looked like he was dressed for a golf outing, stopped to read dates that he connected to the Civil War.

My brother, who had mowed the graveyard lawn as a kid, escorted our mother. A young man with a trumpet stood off to the side. Three ministers arrived after us: two men—one old, one young—and one woman. The white-haired minister was a man my father knew and respected. He was tall and thin, well spoken, conservative and traditional. He was a model for a Rockwell painting that could be titled: "The Minister." The young man was of no consequence, the leader of the new generation of churchgoers. He would not read from *King James.* A lightweight. The woman—my father would never accept a woman in the pulpit, but here she was—I knew.

Mindy and I had gone to the same middle school. She was in my French class. I knew her last name was a French word—a term in music, too. She was a beautiful girl. Sitting near her, nouns, verbs, the past and future tense, fell into a void. Here was a syntax, inflection, tone, accent, and vocabulary worth study. Some boys, already, spoke the language. I could not count to ten.

Once, standing in the gym next to the wooden bleachers that had been pushed up flat against the wall, I heard a guy yell out, "Come on, Mindy, show us that ass!" For a second, I was embarrassed and wanted her to know I was not part of this group and would never say words like that to her, until she smiled and moved her body, fluently, in a way that met the demand. The boys applauded and whistled.

The exchange I'd witnessed, idiomatic and charged with meaning, was more complicated than any use of the subjunctive. But one thing was clear—physical and inchoate: the intent.

It was in Mindy's house one night, no parent in sight, that a girl, not Mindy—but her friend who was also in our class—pinned me down on a leather chair that swiveled back with our weight. It was dark. She kissed me in a foreign way. Suddenly drunk (had I been drinking?), I tried to speak. She pressed a finger to my lips. She brushed the side of her face against mine and whispered in French. The side of my head burned and buzzed—a sensation that surged to the rest of my body. We kissed more. She had told me, literally, to shut my mouth.

Here was Mindy again, at my father's interment ceremony, dressed in a white robe, making her way to me, quickly stepping around raised ground and stone. I had heard she was divorced and remarried. Her own daughter was in high school. Months back, we had talked at the funeral. Now, in the warm sunlight, in the graveyard, we embraced. She kissed me flush on the lips.

> O Mort, vieux capitaine, il est temps! Levons l'ancre
> Ce pays nous ennuie, o Mort! Appareillons!
> Si le ciel et la mer sont noir comme de l'encre,
> Nos coeurs que tu connais sont remplis de rayons! [2]
>
> (Charles Baudelaire, *Flowers of Evil*)

My brother has bad knees, so it was hard for him to get close to the ground. He held one side of the rectangular box, and I held the other. I had held a box like this once before. That box held the remains of my biological father. For him, there had been no interment, no ceremony. The Dragon Lady kept his ashes.

> June 10, 1963. Had a storm last night, but came through with flying colors. Have been sleeping like a baby. I feel so relaxed. The way the ship rolls—it makes you feel like a child in a mother's arms being rocked. The bunk is like a woman's soft dress. So I've slept as if not yet born, feeling again the experience of a fetus in a woman's stomach. I will live in the south of Ireland near Cork. First to England and then to Liverpool the next day. Then it will be time to find a home and to call Hiler to see when I can get over to Paris to see him. Last night it didn't get dark. The midnight sun was on. It was beautiful to see the light of dawn all night. But it was also like a tough time waiting for someone or something to get started. So as not to hold up the sun, I will start painting soon. I still don't know whether to use a curved line or a straight one or to introduce both in the same painting. We will see when the paint and color comes.

The hole had the depth of a hole a kid would dig on his way to China. I recognized the texture of the dirt, the type of rock you'd hit while digging, the bits of root sticking out. A spider crawled into the hole and clung to an inside wall. It was big and

[2] *Oh, Death, old captain, hoist the anchor! Come, cast off!*
We've seen this country, Death! We're sick of it! Let's go!
The sky is black; black is the curling crest, the trough
Of the deep wave; yet crowd the sail on, even so! trans. Edna St. Vincent Millay

had legs like a Daddy Long-Legs, but the body was bigger. It was brown and white-speckled.

We placed the box into the hole. We stood up. My mother took a few steps forward. She spoke perfectly to him. She told us that he had wanted to return to California to see the redwood trees before he died. They had never made the trip. Then she produced two pieces of a redwood tree: one carved and ornate, the other unshaped. She placed them in the hole with the box.

My mother was into religion rather deeply at the time, and every summer we'd rent a house for two or three weeks on Mount Hermon, and we'd stay with friends who owned a house there who were Christian Scientists. They were delightful people. I had a marvelous time. They had a swimming pool and a diving board. The only dive I could do was the jackknife. I did that incessantly. Then we could walk down the railroad tracks through a grove of magnificent sequoia sempervirens, *you know, the big old sequoias. About a mile and a half down the road was a place, something like the Garden of Eden. It was a beautiful place with a stream and a waterfall and a cliff you could jump or dive off. I took a young lady down there to show off my diving. It was the first time I'd been there since the year before. So I got up on the rocks and said, "Watch me!"*

I dived off.

17

January 10, 2008. The next day, I'd fly off for the national conference in New York City. I'd set appointments to meet with presenters at the top of the Hilton Hotel. At one point I would look out a window from the 44th floor and see a segment of the Hudson River framed by canyons of steel.

On Tuesday, at 9:30AM, I'd be back in St. Louis, and I would begin the process of dissolving my marriage to C. We would use a mediator. We would describe our divorce as amicable.

In the fugue of Bach's C major sonata for unaccompanied violin, a simple subject is stated. It is a child humming. But then other voices are added that create tension, power, focus. The violinist must proclaim the life force itself—a gravitational pull in an F-sharp to a massive G-major chord: the Sun.

As I wrote, I listened to Arthur Grumiaux play the piece. It is stained glass. It is architecture. It is a pedal point on D, a chord to fill a church, then the child's theme played upside down with complications to explore: the transmutation of one's pain and one's spirit reaches higher.

How did Grumiaux's father know to give his son Arthur a violin? The church bells in their town rang and the boy knew. *Father, I know their names.* Buy the recording. Listen to the C major fugue. Hear the bells. See the cathedral. Feel a father's recognition of a son's gift. Only the Italian, Antonio Stradivarius, could have made the violin Grumiaux plays. A Strad won't ring for anyone. It requires the hands of a master.

When Mark Rothko painted, he liked his studio to be saturated with music.

Clyfford Still describes Rothko as a chain-smoking Buddha.

Rothko: "I would like to say to those who think of my pictures as serene, whether on friendship or mere observation, that I have imprisoned the most utter violence in every inch of their surface."

C had set the appointment to end our marriage, and, in her practical way, had set therapy appointments for our three boys. But I had not set the date, yet, to visit the Rothkos in St. Louis. Nor had I transcribed my father's tapes up and through his years in the Philippines. What about John Clare? Bruce Chatwin? Melville? Kafka?

In the American art of the 1950s, shouldn't the viewers have looked for the object? Isn't everyone owed an explanation? Why not? Rothko said of a critic, "[he] keeps trying to interpret things he can't understand and which can't be interpreted. A painting doesn't need anybody to explain what it is about. If it is any good, it speaks for itself, and a critic who tries to add to that statement is presumptuous."

I sat at a table with my laptop open, my brain saturated with music. Across from me, a young man placed a piece of muffin on a fork and a young woman opened her mouth, smiling. Her hair was cut like a boy's to frame a pretty face. She beamed love at him.

My lawyer had a walrus mustache. Sagging skin under his eyes: corpse-pale. On his desk: two miniature cannons. On a wall: a sailboat traveled at high speed. He explained the four parts of divorce. He explained how one husband had kept a mistress in high style in a neighboring city. One must be wary of complications.

It was cold in his office and he explained how the building reacted to the change of seasons, the time of day, the wind.

A few days later, C and I met our mediator. The mediator entered numbers into her laptop. A spreadsheet was projected onto a wall. Columns were manipulated, text was wrapped.

"Can a person die from being sad?"

"No, I don't think so," I said to Eli as I tucked him in. The skin above his right eye was swollen from where he got hit earlier that day. A thin red line stretched across the lid behind his glasses. I took his glasses from him, folded them, and carefully placed them on his dresser.

The night before we told Aidan, Eli, and Isaiah that we were getting a divorce, I went to hear a concert: the *tango nuevo* artist, Pablo Zeigler, and his quintet. When I asked C the morning of the concert if she would like to go, she said maybe that would be fun because it would remind her of her days living in Argentina.

In the book she was writing, C used life narratives to explore ideas about identity and geography and space, cities and citizens.

The afternoon before the concert, I emailed C and said that I'd like to go to the concert alone.

The quintet wore black. The guitarist's guitar was blood-red. The vocalist wore red satin. Her skin was white and her thick wavy hair was black and long. The rhythm of a place, the rasp of the bass, the spirit of Astor Piazolla.

I'm in an airport. It is hot and nobody speaks English. The language sounds like silver. I search faces looking for one. When I see her, she recognizes me, but it is different. It has been months. We're transparent like ghosts. We ride a taxi toward the city through ruined towns. When we get up to her apartment, we quickly strip and try to fuck each other into recognition. The sex gives us enough substance to believe in our senses. We are who we think we are, and we are alive in a city near the end of the earth. The pleasures of that place become ours for three months. But I can't stay. We work out an agreement to meet again to be together when she returns. This requires faith on my part, and when I walk away from her in the airport, I don't look back.

In the last piece of the evening, the singer sang the name of the city, over and over.

Buenos Aires, Buenos Aires. Her face expressed pain. Even though I knew the story, I looked back: the apartment on Santa Fe filled with red neon light; the cafes at tea; the high-altitude, sun-blasted towns, a rooster at dawn; the airport where I searched again one last time; a deserted town near Peninsula Valdes; an empty street that led to a dock, a black ship moored, and the open sea at night.

18

In the afterword of James E. B. Breslin's biography of Rothko, he explains why he chose his subject. At the age of forty-four, Breslin had ended up at the Guggenheim Museum where he had been "transfixed, swept up really, by the eloquent simplicity of the paintings that Rothko began to do in 1949." Those paintings struck him as "a visionary alternative to the entanglements" of his daily life. But it was not just that these paintings expressed something "ecstatic," "luminous," "ebullient." Breslin also sensed an "emptiness" that seemed void—"an annihilating vacancy that came from a profound sense of loss."

It was January 2, 1979. Breslin, an English professor, had been in New York City for the M.L.A. convention. He had stayed on a couple of days because the hotel had offered extra days at a low rate. He was in no rush to return to Berkeley where he was about to end a sixteen-year marriage. His emotional response to the paintings that day sparked his interest in Rothko. Seven years later, he started work on the biography. How did Rothko, mid-life, remake his life and art?

That question was worth examining for Breslin, who would remarry and start a new family at the same point in his life. Even more crucial to understand was how and why Rothko—"eminent, wealthy, and productive" in the years that followed—"undid it."

Before Breslin left the museum on that January day, he took a few last turns to circle down the winding ramp to the end of the exhibit: Rothko's "Black on Grey" work from the last year of his life. It was "like a descent into a stark, airless hell."

19

I visited the Basilica Cathedral of St. Louis. It has more than 8,000 shades of color in the mosaics of the vestibule. A father and son team created those mosaics out of 41.5 million pieces of tesserae that cover 83,000 square feet. Each tessera has a background of gold and is covered with a thin layer of glass.

"As you begin your walk," reads a pamphlet, "imagine you are seeing these mosaics as the Byzantines would have seen them...lighted candles and oil lamps...light bouncing off the multi-colored pieces of glass, flickering." Among the images to be found in the mosaics: boy on crutches; dolphin & anchor; globe of the world; headless saint; Jonah & the whale; Saint Louis, King of France; Statue of Liberty; skull; women in white.

Each of the four arches that support the main dome are named: the Arch of Creation (East), the Arch of Sanctification (West), the Arch of Judgment (South), and the Arch of Triumph in Heaven (North).

The director of the Cathedral Concert Series took me around to the organ. He played chords to demonstrate the eight-second reverberation. At his invitation, I had brought my violin. He told me to go to the center under the main dome where sound converged. Layers of arpeggio whirled around me. That's when I looked up and saw in the domed ceiling my son's name in a verse that circled with words about a fiery chariot and fiery horses: *Elias was invited up into heaven.*

When the organ music faded, I put my violin under my chin and played the opening bars of Bach's C major fugue from the *Sonatas and Partitas.* It felt like I was sending the subject into space the way a boy pushes a paper boat onto the surface of a pond. The ripples spread. A banging sound stopped me. Pews were being replaced. I wiped my face and walked back to where the director sat.

The artistry of the mosaics, I read in another pamphlet, provides "a visual lesson in faith, history, art and architecture, a source of inspiration, on many levels, to many visitors from around the world."

20

In the commentary to the *Tibetan Book of The Dead*, Chogyam Trungpa, Rinpoche, says that "the book is not based on death as such, but on a completely different concept of death." He continues:

> It is a *Book of Space.* Space contains birth and death; space creates the environment in which to behave, breathe and act, it is the fundamental environment, which provides the inspiration for this book.

21

The New York Times was left on the table next to me. THIEVES TAKE MASTERWORKS read one caption. It was a cold morning. Patches of snow had yet to melt. Buds were tight in branches. A man told me he had been down with the flu for two weeks—it had taken the energy out of him. Another man wanted to talk to me about what my job was like in sales. At breakfast I read my son's homework assignment. He was supposed to write about his life and eventually connect these twice-a-week writings into a "mini-memoir." In boxes, the teacher had typed up options. One option: family secrets.

The day before, I had read about a moment when the line between sanity and insanity blurs. I should not have read that sentence on that day: a plume of dark smoke right into my forehead. I packed up. My hands shook. Walking home, I had trouble feeling the earth beneath my feet.

Later that day, I explained to a therapist that I was not suicidal. I said I had been studying the life of Mark Rothko for the essay I was writing. Rothko did kill himself. I had just finished the biography and read how he had carefully folded his pants over a chair and how he had done what he had done. She suggested that I probably closely identified with the artist.

Why would one be drawn to another's art? You walk into a museum when you are in your early twenties. Maybe you have just gotten married, and you are starting your life. You have put things back together. Soon, your first child will be born. You sit on a bench that places you in the middle of three paintings. You face one, the other two are in your peripheral vision. Orange, yellow, pinkish-purple. Rectangles. But it is not color. It is not form.

22

Another February morning, I opened *The Castle* and searched dog-ears from when I had read the text in Princeton two years ago. Each time I read, I sat in the same Chinese restaurant on Witherspoon.

> *Ancient sites beckon you to hit the road soon.*
> *Lucky #18, 17, 01, 34, 50, 27*
> *Certains raccourcis causent par fois de long détours.*
>
> *Great thoughts come from the heart.*
> *Lucky #7, 19, 22, 54, 16, 30.*
> *Learn Chinese: Apple (Character) Ping-guo.*
>
> *Luck is coming your way.*
> *Lucky #3, 15, 20, 29, 33, 35*
> *Learn Chinese: Ban-Fa (Character) Method.*

With a black pen, I had marked off one passage on page twenty. Leading up to that passage, K. has just entered the inn, where he sits with two men over beer in the taproom. These men are his assistants: Artur and Jeremias. K. says, while comparing Artur's and Jeremias' faces, that it is difficult to tell them apart, that they are as alike as snakes. At the remark, both smile. K. decides to treat them as one person and call them both Artur.

K. asks Artur to get a sleigh for travel to the Castle for early the next morning. Artur says that it is impossible because no strangers are allowed into the Castle without permission. K. says they will apply for permission by telephone. Artur runs to get a connection to see if K. can go with them to the Castle.

"No," is the answer.

K. attracts attention from the peasants in the inn when he announces that he will telephone himself. The landlord tries to stop them from gathering around K. But they form a tight half-circle at the telephone. The peasants think K. will be unsuccessful.

They must have said things like: "There is no possible way this stranger will get a connection." Or: "Certainly he will be denied permission." Or: "He is a very rude man. He presumes too much." Or: "Did he not hear the first *no*? Maybe on another day, but certainly not today."

K. asks them to be quiet. He has no desire to hear their opinion. I had hatched off the following passage:

> From the mouthpiece came a humming, the likes of which K. had never heard on the telephone before. It was as though the humming of countless childlike voices—but it wasn't humming either, it was singing, the singing of the most distant, or the most utterly distant, voices—as though a single, high-pitched yet strong voice had emerged out of this humming in some quite impossible way and now drummed against one's ears as if demanding to penetrate more deeply into something other than one's wretched hearing.

That humming emanates from Rothko's paintings.

23

February 29, 2008. Rothko's paintings were somewhere in St. Louis. Viewers stopped by to look. Rothko's paintings were also in New Haven. The Yale Museum had re-opened. *The Castle* was at the house. Same for *Moby-Dick* and the other texts. In one month I'd move out.

"How's your project coming along?" That was what my neighbor asked me. He knew I wrote.

My neighbor's wife was German, and I liked listening to her speak English. It was better when she spoke German to her sons. Then they paid attention. My neighbors were good people. They made sure their boys knew how to play several instruments.

Maybe I was too shaky from the divorce to go on. Walk the deck with Melville? Secure a sleigh to travel to a castle I'd never reach? Write a fugue in words? I had no rules to follow. I was closer to the other definition. I was the husband who was found many weeks later in another city wandering the streets. He didn't know who he was. He had no wallet, no ID.

I stared into a tall mirror at the end of a row of tables. My laptop screen had a backlit white apple. The apple glowed in the center of the chest of a darkened figure.

24

March 20, 2008. My neighbor told me it was the strangest spring in St. Louis in seventeen years. Buds had yet to open. It rained and it was cold. My real estate agent called with updates.

I propped open my old laptop and hoped it would start-up. It held writing from when we had lived in New Haven, when I had taught in Bridgeport. The computer was heavy like stone. It was black. Next to it, the white one. The screens grew large. Mozart's "Kyrie" from his *Mass in C Minor* filled the room.

I took my seat. I couldn't move. Some of the people smelled, one man in particular, loud and full of opinions about the nature of crime and violence, sweated through shirt sleeves with the same concentrated hatred he felt for the accused. It was a military operation: he had seen it himself back in the war, the way the accused had left his house with his two compadres, at even distances, the one in front a lookout, signaling back to the other two with a beep of his car alarm.

I had trouble focusing. When we reassembled, I realized that, again, I had chosen poorly: I leaned to one side and sniffed the back of my hand.

I felt nauseated when I looked at the accused. Often our eyes met, perhaps, I thought, because we were the same age. Aside from me, only senior citizens had been able to serve. Even the judge had white hair and strained to hear testimony. When he left the courtroom, he listed to the left.

The courtroom was like a crypt. An armed guard slumped next to a panel in the wall that lead to the judge's chambers. A wooden figure decorated the judge's desk: a man in a top hat who balanced on point like a ballerina.

The prosecutor had a milky complexion and looked as though he never needed to shave. He was soft but methodical: a good doctor of justice, a lethal injection in an air-conditioned room. The disgust he felt for having to take time to explain the obvious guilt of the accused surfaced in a sarcastic grin, arms folded, head tilted back as he beseeched the track lighting in the courtroom ceiling.

The attorney for the accused would have won easily if the proceedings had been reduced to a fight. Testosterone, thick mustache, he tucked his shirt back in after his chest expanded during a heated retort. When contradicted, he could barely contain his rage, which found inadequate catharsis as he flexed in his hand-tailored suit. To crush hostile witnesses with his fist would have been preferable, but instead he put one hand on his hip, moved the other to smooth his mustache, and, again, asked the witness to recall what was forgotten: "If ya can."

I looked away when they passed around photographs of the deceased: entry wounds, exit wounds, information imparted by an expert witness with whom the judge seemed delighted. She wore the traditional dress of her native country.

When the photographs were gone, I looked up: on the prosecutor's desk a few feet away, an image of a man's head. It had been shaved bald in one spot to expose the hole. The face was narrow and ashen, the lips turned down.

When we were sequestered, I read a story. I learned where the protagonist lived and about his aspirations to be a painter—then two quick knocks, and we filed back to our seats.

I realized, as cardboard displays were paraded in front of us, that the prosecutor was intent on establishing that a certain place existed at a certain time in the past: architectural drawings, maps, photographs from the ground, photographs from the air. Often he would rest the exhibit on an artist's easel and begin, using colored pens, to draw: lines along streets, circles in front of a house, an asterisk in an empty lot.

A conflict developed, things we should not be allowed to hear, and we were again sent out. The story was gone. So I pulled from my briefcase a yellow notepad. After I had written a few sentences, we were called back in.

More evidence: dried stains on the flap of a baseball cap, bottles of beer in a bag. I cupped my hands like a beggar, and the old man next to me deposited in them two objects that looked like teeth. They were heavy, though, and coated with a white powder that came off on the tips of my fingers and then dissolved as I rubbed them together. The record was augmented to note that the white substance was the powdered skull of the deceased.

We left. In the waiting room again, I wrote a story with its own courtroom scene. I use the word "cobblestone." The prosecutor in my story had taken photographs of a street, a close-up of a trolley-car. He'd acquired audio-tape of a sound like thunder. Transcripts of conversations. He called his first witness, a stocky man, whose bushy eyebrows formed triangles above his eyes. He stood and took the oath. The stenographer asked him to repeat his name, and he informed her that his name could not be pronounced in English. As he sat down, he reached up to adjust the microphone, and then produced a hard roll of bread from his pocket. The judge requested that he not eat in court.

"All right, all right," he said. He explained that he was involved in the creation of the first atomic bomb and that he had spent several years at an institute for the advancement of human thought. He wore a medallion that resembled a sand-dollar, and the prosecutor asked him what it was.

“It is used for time travel.” He giggled.

The judge warned him that he was under oath, and he was to tell the truth, or there would be consequences. At this, the witness leveled a camera and clicked a picture of the judge, which resulted in his removal.

We were called back to the nonfiction courtroom.

The next witness approached the stand in baby steps. He stated his name and took the oath. He testified that he had lived at a certain address during the time in question.

“What were you doing that evening?”

“Dishes. Nah, nah, wait a minute. I was in the bedroom, then I went to the kitchen.”

“What were you doing in the bedroom?”

“Can’t say.”

“What do you mean?”

“I just can’t say.”

“Sir, may I remind you that you are under oath and that your failure to testify may add time to your sentence.”

“Look, I told you. I can’t say. It’s *personal.*”

The prosecutor rouses the judge whose hand has begun to sink into his face as though it were putty.

“Answer the question.”

“Nah, I can’t.”

“Answer the question.”

“I told you already, it’s personal.”

“Answer the question.”

“No.”

“Sir, need I remind you where you are?”

Stifled laughter. The witness grins.

"All right," the prosecutor says, "forget that for moment. You made a sworn statement saying you heard shots that night, am I right?"

"Ummm."

"Louder, please."

"Yes."

"I want you to tap out the rhythm of the shots on the stand there, if you will."

The witness hits the side of the stand with his fist three times.

"Would you describe the sounds you heard as popping sounds?"

"Nah, they was more like 'BLOOM!'"

"Now, you have also testified that you saw three shadows run beneath your kitchen window."

"Ummm."

"Please speak directly into the mic."

"Yes."

"Now, I want you to think back. There is a tree, is there not, in front of the parking lot, visible from the kitchen window during the day?"

"Yup."

"Is that tree, strike that. Was that tree visible from the kitchen window that night?"

"Yeah, naw, naw, wait a minute...yeah."

"Do I need to get the tapes of your original statements to refresh your memory?"

"Huh?"

"To *remind* you of what you said, remember, when the officer took your statement."

"You mean Snowball?"

"Yes, when the officer known as Snowball took your statement. Do you need us to play the tape?"

"Nah."

"Then, now think back to that night. Could you see that tree from your kitchen window? Yes or no?"

"Yes."

"Yes?"

"Definitely, yes."

"Your honor, may I have a minute?"

With great frustration, the prosecutor goes to his desk and shuffles through a pile of photographs. His assistant helps him find the shot. He snatches it and displays it so that everyone can see a grainy image of nothing. He says, righteously, "This is a photograph taken from the kitchen at night, several days after the night in question. Do you see a tree?"

"Naw…yeah!...that's not what I'm saying."

"What, exactly, are you saying?"

"What I'm sayin' is I know it's there, know what I mean, like you can sense it's out there right near the edge of the lot. I mean, it's always been right there, know what I'm sayin'?"

Snow blew like white ash in a frenzy.

The poorly lit room, the science teacher whose curly hair barely hid her scalp, the way she gripped a piece of paper. I had tried to see to the front, between the heads, necks, and shoulders. At some point, I had hoped, they would move into place like tumblers in a lock, to allow an unobstructed view to the casket. Organ music had swelled through a vent above my head.

I glided along a newly paved street past a marsh. It required no exertion, and as I increased speed, I realized if I lifted my arms away from my sides, my body would lift. The ascent was rapid as I traveled through space shoulder high with the tops of green trees and I arched my back into a cloudless sky a stiff breeze in my face. A current entered my body through my palms. Above the trees the voltage began to surge: thin branches of light crackling, twisting, flashing, popping, smoking my arms.

25

O thin men of Haddam,
Why do you imagine golden birds?
(Wallace Stevens, "Thirteen Ways of Looking at a Blackbird")

26

A Year Before My Biological Father's Death

An incision from throat to belly.
The cracking of the breast plate.
An incision from groin to ankle; the taking of vein.
The re-routing, the quintuple bypassing.
The long fissure of a wound, eighty staples closing.
A ventilator.
The removal of a tube.
A room with a view of Puget Sound.
The black ink drying before the watercolor.
A biker, heavy tattoos, angelic demonic, with a pocket camera.
Meticulous, a VCR, maps in drawers—a murderer, retired.
A getaway car with two sentinels at an international airport.
The art of cussing in cigarette clouds.
Catching sunfish in the mind.
The totem pole, the dock, the ferry, and starfish—muscular, big as dogs.
A squadron of ladybugs landing high above the Hood Canal.
A misdiagnosed growth.
Malignant fuel for flight.
A riddle of absence.
A cup of coffee, no appetite.
A waitress with gray eyes affectionately punching the wrong man.
The same sentence in three languages.
The broken speed limit, the last car on the ferry.
Throwing away pills.
A salmon bursting silver shrapnel.
To see again only in dreams.
Fishing tackle sold.
A bridge brought down by storm.
A geography of insight tracing the Olympic Peninsula.
A phalanx of pines, hushed, towering.
The machine.
A conviction.
A sentence.
A VA home.
This room: toilet, TV, desk, bed.
Waiting for an eye to open.

27

October 21, 1963. Now I am drunk. I don't like it, but I will wake another day God willing. If not, a long sleep. If only the end could be as easy. I will sleep forever. I feel hopeless. But if there is one for me, I will know more than being torn apart. Time alone will be the judge. I am strained from the lack of mental and emotional control to deal with people. To be a stone or to be a flesh-eating thing. No answer, no answer. Just a thought: I will learn much from these trips to the insane—but can I use it? There is not enough space on a canvas—things must be fuller, bigger, stronger, almost monstrous. It's got to get out, and get you out into you, into the air, alive. It is not enough to just paint something. You must breathe life into it. Your life. I realize I have been living a life I don't have. When I paint, I know it. You live, but you don't. You pass and become the past.

28

April 10, 2008. Pink and white blossom. It rained. Drops beaded and rolled off umbrellas. Cars lined up. A woman waited. On her enormous calf she had had an eye tattooed with the word SERENITY scripted below. My hands shook as I typed.

I sat in a soundproof booth. A series of beeps of varying pitch and loudness.

I formed zero after zero in the wrong squares of a deposit slip.

Near the end of a day in a hospital, I met a doctor who was of Indian descent. She told me people hallucinate and run the halls. They need to be restrained.

I read that Rothko's children were going to exhume his remains and move them to a Jewish cemetery to be next to his wife.

29

A recovered fragment from an early draft of *Just a Life*:

> I was going into New York to hear Bill play at the Vanguard. Bill told me he couldn't read music until he was in his twenties, and he thought Aidan, who had great trouble reading music, was a jazz pianist. To help Aidan with note recognition, I had bought flashcards, and I had joked with Bill, that for his edification, I was going to bring a card into the city for him.

Onto a flashcard, I had copied Clare's poem "I Am," which was written while Clare was an inmate at the North Hampton General Lunatic Asylum. The musical note *A* I had fitted into the word "soaring" from the fourth line:

Of dullness and my soaring thoughts destroyed.

I had traced the word "creation" from the eleventh line around the bottom of the G-Clef:

Tracing creation, like my maker, free,—

30

We rented out a place in Sunset Studios—we had a gorgeous reception room with a grand piano, two offices, a private bathroom, and I made arrangements to work with clients I'd worked with before like Papermate Pens, Starkist Tuna, Pacific Intermountain Express, Wells Fargo Bank, Rheingold Beer. I had worked with Peggy Lee, Hoagy Carmichael, everybody—they were all singing [sings]*: "My beer is Rheingold, the dry beer, tuh dah da dah da dah."*

We made lots of money, but I wanted to do my own thing. I was just producing commercials for clients. I had no creative outlet, nothing to do with how to construct the thing. I could do it in my sleep.

One day an editor whom I knew named Lucky Brown came along and said, "Bob, I'm gonna get you out of all this." He had this guy, Jo Jo Joseph, who was reputedly the Number 2 man in the second largest motion picture studios in the Philippines. They had an investor, a rice grower in a little province who wanted to get into the motion picture industry, but they had to come up with something that he was interested in doing. So I came up with the idea of doing The Tales of Marco Polo. They wanted a deal with an American producer to come over and shoot a picture there, using their facilities, they'd pay all local costs, and we had to put up-front money for the American actors, transportation to and from, final edit.

So I mortgaged the house, sold one of the cars, told Billie [his first wife] *about it—it was not a discussion. Up to that point we had no problem with money. She had started drinking, but not too heavily at that point. I needed the money for our travel over there and had to pay an actor.*

I'd called a friend of mine, Meyer Mishkin, and I said I needed a very Lincolnesque guy, who can ride a horse, handle a sword, and what have you. So he sent me Dick Garland who was the ex-husband of Beverly Garland who was a better-known actor than he was. He looked the part, but he had a laugh like a horse's whinny, he'd never held a sword, he was afraid of horses—but I didn't find that out until we got there. So

I said good-bye to my children and wife and we took off for the Philippines.

The film was an idea I just made up entirely out of whole cloth. As soon as Jo Jo told me his people loved the idea and wanted to participate as co-producers, I started writing. By the time I got to the Philippines I had six chapters written, scrawled, scribbled. Nothing in cement. I'd never done anything like that in my life. All I did was make commercials and directed a few live television programs or produced them, but I did not have the experience to write, cast, direct a motion picture. I just did not have the ability, but I was a young genius. I was going to make motion picture history and lots of money and fame and fortune.

Lucky, who was the editor, was also going to act the part of Marco Polo's foil—a Sancho Panza type of role. I re-wrote history. I did not write that Marco Polo had his father and his uncle with him on his trip, but none of the history helped at all. I just made it up, entirely.

We arrived in the Philippines in 1957, landed in Manila to great fanfare: banners, people from the press and newspapers, 3 television stations. Albert [Jo Jo's brother] *had circulated to the press that he, at great cost, had obtained the services of one of Hollywood's greatest writers, producers, directors, and a famous actor, Richard Garland—he'd actually just done a bunch of TV shows, just walk-ons and 3 lines on big shows—but we were feted and celebrated.*

So we cast about, looked for locations, and found that the Philippines' most famous actor/producer had died because his dog had contracted rabies and bit him on the ass, and he died, and his fans rent their clothes and cried and screamed and a cortege of 30 cars with floral bouquets and kinds of crap—it was a big funeral, he was a big star—he had a studio. It was a building made of cement blocks, it was 40 feet wide by 80 to 110 feet long, and that was it. Nothing in it. Everything had been stolen or sold by the grieving widow who did not get much money because he had blown it in lawsuits and paternity suits, so she was glad to rent us the studio.

The studio had walls 30 feet high but there was a 2-foot gap between the walls and the ceiling because it was hot, no air-conditioning, and that was how they let the wind in. It was fresh air, but you could not work in that because you had an echoing building, and the sounds of the outside world crept in. Everybody kept fighting cocks in the Philippines, everybody was riding a Vespa, and the kids were playing and screaming and yelling and the cocks were crowing. So we had to close it up. Then we couldn't work because the temperature and humidity were such that you couldn't work without breaking a sweat, make-up running down the face of the performers, ruining costumes. But I knew I was going to be successful, I knew it in my heart of hearts. I was an asshole at the time, I didn't know anything, but with a little luck I would have, but it did not turn out that way.

We cast for Kubla Kahn, his court, and a love interest. I did not know if Marco had ever had one, and I didn't care. So we cast for a girl that I named in the script By Yu Ling—which I was told meant White Jade Blossom. I guess every woman in the Philippines wanted to be an actress because we had over 300 women standing in the hot sun waiting to be tested for the part.

We had gone up to where MacArthur had made his landing on the far northern shore and found a wonderful area, nobody around, and we slipped some money to the local people that worked for the highway department and got them to make us a desert. It was sandy up there with sand dunes 30-40 feet high and about 150 yards long and 60-70 yards wide: a great Gobi Desert. We shot some stuff up there in Kubla's court where Marco was first introduced to Kubla Kahn, and we'd done a decent job with the studio: full marble pillars, walls covered with faux marble paper, all made there—the Filipinos could make anything out of string and spit, they had to, that was the way they worked.

So we had a pretty damned decent court scene, and we had a couple of good shots. I had a pool built—I don't know if Kubla Kahn had a pool in his palace, but I wanted a pool, so we made one about 3 feet deep and it leaked. We had to hire people to keep mopping it up so people wouldn't fall on their asses. We put blue dye in the water to hide the obvious deficiency. I never wrote a scene around that pool.

Our first shot was about 2 1/2 months after we got there. I finally found my By Yu Ling, we did scenes in the desert, and I had to build everything out of bamboo—a 25 foot high camera position where I, as the director, would stand and direct. If I had had puttees I would have worn them. I had a sound powered horn. And for the first day we were there, Changor the Bandit and Marco were practicing a dueling scene and Changor was not happy with the aluminum swords we had provided. Unbeknownst to me, he had brought his own, and he cut Dick's finger off, almost entirely to the bone, it was just hanging there. I was up there when I heard the screaming and crying. I had to make a decision. Either I was going to be a sonofabitch or ruin the whole thing, blow all the money, so I chose to be a sonofabitch. So we took him to a doctor, stitched and bandaged him up, and we went on.

The T.N.T. Boys were marvelous, young, bright Filipino men who could put anything together. I had asked Totoy to arrange for rockets to be fired off because the Chinese had invented them and used them in battle. He said he could do that.

They had also constructed five yurts. A yurt was a Mongol tent made out of felt from yaks and camels and for all I know horses and dogs, it's round, conical, with one entrance. We assembled townspeople, cast women, men, no children, and the script called for us, meaning Marco Polo, to attack this little town and because they hadn't paid their taxes, he was to kill all the men and rape all the women. Kubla Kahn had sent Marco to do it.

So we set up to shoot. I got Marco and Lucky to brandish their swords and run into the firefight—I had some fires going—and at whatever point that I thought it was appropriate, I yelled, "Totoy, fire off the rockets!" And he did. Except the T.N.T. Boys just lit off a bunch of sparklers, the kind kids have in their hands at the Fourth of July when they're not allowed firecrackers.

"Hold! Cut! What the hell are you doing?"

"We're shooting rockets, Mr. Bob."

"Those are not rockets. Those are sparklers. You know, rockets go BockBOOM! And then there are big sparks."

"Oh, yes sir, Mr. Bob, you mean BockPOOMS! Those are rockets in the Philippines."

"Can we get some of these?"

"Well, I can probably make them tonight and we can shoot tomorrow maybe, sir."

"For sure?"

"Well, that is maybe almost for sure, sir."

So we broke the company and went back to Manila.

The next afternoon, we set up for the evening and soon as it was dark, the rockets went off, and they were indeed rockets. It looked great, and I was very happy. Everybody rushed around brandishing swords and screaming and yelling and having fights. It was just delightful. At least that's what I had meant it to be, so when I got as much footage as I thought I needed I yelled, "Cut!"

Everything stopped except some screaming that was going on. I thought, "Jesus, is somebody hurt?" So I ran up the little hill over where the tents were. Well, the B.A.D. Boys, who were another group of extras we had hired, had misunderstood my directions. I had not given them in Tagalog. It was a terrible mistake. I had not had them translated. When I said they were to rape the women, they thought that was what I wanted—so that's what they were doing to the women in the yurts. I had a sudden image of me being impaled on swords or bulldozed by husbands or whatever, fathers, so I tried to calm them down. At that point, Jo Jo came up with handfuls of pesos and gave them to the women and paid them off. They seemed very happy and said they were having more fun and getting paid better than their normal jobs. As it turned out, most of them were prostitutes from one of the clubs in Manila.

31

September 19, 1963. I'm in Paris. Don't ask why. Drank too many beers and found myself on a train. I'm in Montparnasse to see Hiler. Went to his house but no one came to answer. I'll stay up tonight and see if I can find him in the morning. So now a cig and a French beer—not bad. The meal on the train was something else: soup then curry-rice, fish, potatoes, roast beef then wine all the time, bread all the time, more on anything you want, then coffee, cheese, fruit. I still have an orange with me for breakfast. Paris. It's now a little after 4AM. I am hungry. Cup of coffee and a salami sandwich till 8:30AM and at 9AM to see if Hi is there. If not, to the Louvre or to a hotel to sleep. I walked from Montparnasse to the Seine and back. Not bad. Not good. I don't seem to be so taken by Paris.

September 24, 1963. I've been through four or five days of hell. I can't go into it. I can't write what happened when I met Hiler. Anyway, I am still in Holland and finished a good drawing today. I will feel better tomorrow. I am working and thinking.

September 30, 1963. I've finished four or five paintings in the last six days. I have twelve canvases on order and four ready to go in the studio and have broken into an insane painting free and crazy and it's great. At this pace I'll have a hundred canvases. I hope it will sustain itself. It is a little hard on me, but I don't care. I'm going to paint this afternoon and work on another tonight: yellow and flowers and fruit and pure hues and heavy paint and fast strokes, honest me, open to see and open to feel and full of whatever it will be, good or bad flowing over at the brim, and mental as a jaybird and love it, fuck you, fuck me. HAHAHA!

October 14, 1963. I have reached a new low in despair—a depression of a sort that I still have some regard for myself but a feeling of aloneness, and I can't go to anyone. I have no family, although they may bury me. I don't want to drive myself to paint, but it seems my only salvation. I don't want to be drunk again. I am sick in my guts from too much drink, as my mother called it. What can liberate me from myself—you, my son. Coffee. Sleep. Painting. I don't know or want to know. If I had a dog, I would give it away. Same day, now 12:30PM. I just finished the self-portrait. I'm having a beer. You look at it. See what you think. I don't know how to say what I do. So look at it—please. Find what you can see with your own eyes.

32

January 13, 1964. The money came. I've been sick from drinking. Today, I made a step in the right direction. I had breakfast and dinner and no beer. I want to go home. I wrote Pat for a loan—hope it works out, and I'll leave in two months if it does. My second son was born on the 21st of December in Los Angeles. Now everything is double. Even my loneliness. So what else matters? Since I last wrote on the 8th of December, I have done many paintings. I think I'll work tonight. I have not painted for almost two weeks. Like I said, I've been sick. Sometimes I can't even think to think, but I can always drink. *The Days of Wine and Roses* could take a good lesson from this poor character when I am drunk. Maybe when I die, they will say it was a shame he didn't paint more. At times it doesn't seem important. At times, nothing seems important. But tomorrow always seems to come, even if it is not important. Like a bad penny—whatever that is.

At the end of my biological father's journal, three paragraphs form an incomplete letter to a friend. I like to think the letter is for me.

Anyway, my problems have been personal ones. I fight with myself to do and make the right moves, the right work, and the right decisions. Alone, these things seem insurmountable, but because of you and your help, it was possible, and it is possible for me to continue to work under conditions that before might have stopped my production. Or just stopped me. I think you understand from our talks in Hollywood and Ireland. I am sure it will be clear when we meet again.

I will return to LA with more work than I expected, both oil and watercolor. Before any of the paintings go to a gallery for showing, they are all at your disposal to pick whatever you like. I will be honest to our bargain and will never be less than the man you trusted.

What is most valuable to all men is time to learn more of themselves and time to understand living and time to grow within and without unaffected by outside forces if possible, and to only do battle with themselves. Many men are too involved with the day-to-day and never get this chance to go outside themselves to see what is going on inside. To miss this is in many cases a sad and slow destruction of the man himself. For me, your friendship and trust have given me this chance, and it is important for you to know that this important help from you made my work this year possible. I hope in that work you will see this feeling of progression and love and understanding, which came out of our relationship. I hope they will give you the feeling of your being part of them. But I hope too, from just plain looking, they will give you a visual satisfaction. I find it difficult to explain in a

DAY OF THE DOLPHIN

I finished the first twenty pages of *Walden.* I was doing what I'd asked my students to do—to keep a journal as they read twenty pages a day. In eighth hour, there was not a little grumbling about that. One student, Adrienne, started to protest, and thought I should be taxed for requiring them to read so much. Yes, I had assigned a lot—the ongoing author project, a creative nonfiction essay (whatever *that* was), all due Monday.

I used a broken incense burner to clamp down the first pages of *Walden—two years and two months,* Thoreau says, he lived there. Two students in eighth hour said they'd been to Walden Pond. Both swam in it. John (the other was Rachel) said he went inside the hut and may have, somewhere, a picture. I asked him to bring the picture in. Earlier in that class, I had gone up and down the rows (twenty-five students in rows of five—although on that day Kate was sick and Isabella was at a debate tournament) with an annotated copy of Thoreau's book open to a page with a photo.

"He looks like Lincoln."

"Why'd he grow his beard *that* way?"

On page one, I circled the word *obtrude*; I'd underlined *in this it will be retained*—referring to Thoreau's claim that in most books, the *I* is omitted, but he'd keep it for his book. And then more underlining: *Moreover, I, on my side, require of every writer, first or last, a simple and sincere account of his own life, and not merely what he has heard of other men's lives; some such account as he would send...these pages are more particularly addressed to poor students.*

During that class, Rachel tried to get me to do my dolphin impersonation again. But I said no. The students said it was a bad impersonation—it *was* bad—but I sometimes felt the need to let the absurd into my classroom, and I told them, in mock earnestness, that if I were to travel to the coast of Florida, give the call, dolphins would literally jump out of the ocean to greet me.

I had also told them, at the beginning of the class, that I had streamlined my plans: the daily quotation, then biographical info on Thoreau, then I'd give them time to add details from their reading of the bio the night before, and then: reading. The reading part went well in fifth hour—only 13 in that one (although Meghan was absent—"probably out saving the world," said Graham, and Coraline was also debating). It was quiet in that room. At one point, (I read, too) a student said, "If he ate no flesh, what did he eat?" Beans. Lots of beans. Part 7 is called "The Bean Field."

In eighth hour, the room would let out a sound at auspicious moments. The sound was similar to the sound of a high-pitched fart—the pitch slowly lowering. The room had commented on Hawthorne, Poe, Franklin, Shakespeare, Homer—and, of course, the room had commented plenty on my teaching. On Friday, Thomas (a young Contrarian), kept arguing about the location of the Sandwich Islands, which lead to a confrontation with Rachel who needed *real* quiet to read—and as I tried to quiet them both down so that they all could get back to reading, the room let one out.

Near the end of eighth hour, Laurel walked up and asked if she could go to the nurse because she had a migraine. She looked washed out—very pale—her blonde hair did not hide the welt near the back of her neck.

"Sure—just write out a pass and I'll sign it."

I went back to reading. I sat Indian-style, in front of the classroom, beneath the SMART Board, the oversized computer "touch screen" that was supposed to take the place of the dry-erase board that took the place of the chalk board in suburban schools—eventually the SMART Board would make its way, piecemeal, into the inner-city classrooms. I had never used the SMART Board (I'd eventually get in trouble for that, I was sure), but I had wondered aloud to my students if I was as smart as the SMART Board, or its makers, or the younger generation of teachers who tap its surface, the light from the board reflected in the students' uniform gaze, their collective mouth agape. Teaching should be a picture show. Aren't we all now visual, screen-bound learners?

On page three—*He has not time to be anything but a machine.* I made a note to connect this to Bartleby, who, I supposed, reacted against being a copy machine, a scrivener, as much as Melville reacted against having to write prose that would sell. I had also written the name Marx. At one point, a few weeks earlier, I included in seminar notes to my students a dense paragraph from Marx's *The Alienation of Labor*—that was while they had been reading *Bartleby* and learning about Melville.

As they read in fifth hour, I got the class's attention to read aloud: *The mass of men lead lives of quiet desperation.* I told the students there were many famous lines one could find—maybe they'd get a sense for them as they read. I'd introduced what an aphorism was (while they read Emerson's essays) and converted that noun on the dry-erase board into an adjective and said that a writer could have an aphoristic style—like Emerson: *God will not have his work made manifest by cowards.*

"Emerson just jumps around from topic to topic," said one student.

"He's a hypocrite," said another.

"He *said* he would contradict himself," said a third.

I said I appreciated what they all were saying because they had identified something quintessentially American—it was like jazz—taking a European form, getting improvisational with it, being willfully wrong, even. I made air quotes around the word "wrong."

"Isn't an essay supposed to prove an idea, you know, put evidence together to make a point?"

"Exactly."

In his hut, or in Emerson's home, or wherever he was in time and space, Thoreau writes, *One generation abandons the enterprises of another like stranded vessels.*

During the biographical part of the lesson, I said, "If I were Thoreau, I'd already be dead for two years. He only lived to be forty-four."

"But on the biography you gave us, someone had written forty-five. *Someone* can't add."

"True—but it is really forty-four." I didn't tell them I copied the information out of my colleague's copy of *The Norton Anthology of American Literature.* I remembered seeing the number 45 she'd written and circled in black. The imprecision of teaching was a worthy topic. All I aimed for was to know for certain what I didn't know and to know that I knew what I knew.

I was still in the first section called Economy. *It would be well,* Thoreau writes, perhaps, *if we were to spend more of our days and nights without any obstruction between us and the celestial bodies, if the poet did not speak so much from under a roof, or the saint dwell there so long.* Thoreau says he begins to occupy his house on the Fourth of July, and he calculates that in materials, his house cost him $28 12 ½. I didn't know what the half meant—I'd have to look that up in an annotated version. In the meantime, I had fallen behind on the reading schedule I'd set up for my students, and I'd have to get up early the next day to get through the next twenty pages.

Instead of reading it all when I should have, K cut my hair while I sat on a wooden chair in the tub, and then we took the kids out to see K's mother. For a few minutes, we were in a Macy's because K's mother was buying me a watch. That was part of a Korean custom—the mother-in-law buys the new son-in-law a nice watch. It was supposed to involve a suit and shoes, but K and I had both been married before, so it was being reduced to the watch. Macy's was all red paper wrapping and bows and white lights. I tried to block it out, pick the watch, and get out. In the restaurant afterwards, my second son made too much of a fuss about getting fried ice cream. Two women walked by our table wearing vibrant red, pink, and white *hanbok*, a momentary image from another century, another place—they headed toward the karaoke bar, and the background thumping got louder for a second, and then softened.

Fifth hour was reading. I had shown them John's photos of and around Walden Pond and everyone liked them. Emerson's massive tombstone at Sleepy Hollow Cemetery (as though the Oversoul pooped a big rock)—that got the best reaction.

Angelica just did not like Emerson as much as Thoreau. Thoreau was less pretentious—which perhaps was reflected in the photos of the two tombstones—Thoreau's just said HENRY. It was small, like the heel of a loaf of bread. A pinecone was next to it, and someone had left little stones and a large white egg. What was that? An ostrich egg? The students were zipping up, packing up. The announcement sound had gone off and a voice said, "Sorry for the interruption…if you hear the fire alarm go off, please prepare to ignore it." Then the alarm went off. Then another announcement, "Please disregard the fire alarm." We all laughed. A student said, "My shin still hurts."

I read some of pages 61–80 the night before and then on the morning of December 7th, I read more. I needed to look up the words *alluvion* and *d'appui*. The line *Time is but the stream I go a-fishing in* popped up. I'd use that for the daily quote and beneath it write Emerson's formulation: *Man is a stream whose source is hidden.* I'd read part of an essay called "The Growth of the Soul: Coleridge's Dialectical Method and Strategy of Emerson's *Nature*," and I'd read some of it aloud to my students, how critics of the past had trouble, how *Nature* does "confuse the mind" and how "one cannot always penetrate its rapid-cross of ideas and see its underlying intention."

During class, I checked students' journals. After the line about fishing in time, Thoreau drinks in that stream, sees the sandy bottom, detects how shallow it is, and when the thin current slides away, eternity remains. Then he goes deeper: he fishes in the sky whose bottom is pebbly with stars, which he cannot count. Then Thoreau knows not the alphabet to count the stars/pebbles. Finally, he compares his intellect to a cleaver that can rift its way into the secrets of things—and then his head is an organ for burrowing, and he wants to burrow into hills to find the richest vein, which is somewhere hereabouts. He begins to mine, and so did I. *Yes, I can invert the stream and use my hands and feet to get to those hills. Will my students?* I thought so—and I didn't think a teacher was necessary. Weren't the students' journal entries as valid as my own—I wondered if they knew. Maybe I could do for my students what my father did for me. When I was ten, my father and I had gone saltwater fishing, and we had to use sandworms—horrible things, really, out of some horror movie: orange, writhing, with pincers. We had a box of them, the type of carton you'd get from a Chinese take-out. My father cut them (not that that stopped their attack on his hand), baited the hook, and those worms curled and pinched around the hook on which they had just been double-impaled. I walked out with my rod and Zebco reel, careful not to slip on the slick jetty rocks, found a secure spot, and cast out.

On the night K cut my hair, I drew myself up close to her in our bed. Before I drifted with her into the ocean of sleep, I heard my father's voice, an aural hallucination, but I was so tired I just kept listening to the voice as though it was nothing out of the ordinary. When my father stopped talking, I realized I had been hearing my father's voice, his actual voice, and felt throughout my body how much I missed him—the need to share what had happened these past few years since his death—the divorce, the estrangement from my oldest son. The last time I had heard his voice, I had been jogging the boardwalk at Ocean City, just after his death and before the divorce, and I figured that was the way grief worked.

"You have to learn to bait your own hook," he once told me, joking serious, as he drove me back to college. And then, I remembered in class that it was Pearl Harbor Day, and I said it was the day that would live in infamy, but for my father, who was 16 on that day in 1941, it was just a day where he had been in the back seat of a car in Oakland, California, necking with a girl named Sally Fitzpatrick when the announcement came over the radio. Angelica said that the girl's name sounded out of *The Catcher in the Rye.* I agreed—a combination of a few literary names in that one. As I thought more about it, my father may have said Sally Girlpatrick. Who knows if the name is correct? At sixteen, my father said he was not allowed to enlist, but he eventually made it in, and found himself heading towards Hawaii, and then to an island called Iwo Jima. When he was finally taken off that island for medical care, he was only a year older than my students. Hand-to-hand combat had been a formative experience for my father. For my students: texting and touch-screens.

It was December 8th. 7:34AM. The PLC (Professional Learning Community) meeting was supposed to start five minutes ago and the assistant superintendent with her thick strand of pearls was walking the halls. Better be alert.

I had completed up to page 100 that morning. But I did not have time to write a journal entry. Pam (she taught the other sections of HAL—Honors American Literature) showed up, and we got to work on our review packet and final exam. Pam shared her final review—she would give students sample questions like:

Lost his/her audience when he/she stopped writing seafaring adventures and turned to writing novels that explored deep philosophical issues through extensive use of allegory and symbolism.

Students were supposed to match:

A. Thomas Jefferson B. Benjamin Franklin C. Nathaniel Hawthorne D. Edgar Allan Poe E. Herman Melville F. Ralph Waldo Emerson

For our "common assessment" questions (a mandate from central office), students would identify quotations. One from the review:

Trust thyself: every heart vibrates to that iron string.

Well, I thought it came from…wait—didn't I underline that in Emerson? Yes, it sounded like "Self-Reliance." Fine. We ended our session with Pam telling me about a colleague having marriage troubles.

"Adam, can I ask you. I mean, I'm not a man. But as a man, do you think that Susie is attractive?"

As a man? What? I hedged—"Well, to many men, if a woman appears to be under thirty, then maybe they think she's attractive. Plus, she has long hair."

Laughing in a strangely conspiratorial tone that made me tense, Pam said, "And I know you can't say this, but she has big breasts."

I tried to play it off. I said trouble can occur when a couple is not in agreement about having children.

"That's what I think, too."

Speaking of how having children was no guarantee, I added a comment about my oldest son, about how hard it was when the other divorced parent undercuts.

Pam then told me how her daughter went to a party when the parents were not there. I knew this terrain. She told me how she handled it. While she talked, I could only think about how she had no idea what was really going on with her daughter and how parents tell stories to themselves to stay comfortable.

The meeting ended, and I realized, clearly, that I'd have to write the final from scratch and make the quotation identification thing work for the common assessment—even if I had covered slightly different material. Fine. Class time on PLC days was cut short, so my classes mostly analyzed the daily quote: *The works of the great poets have never yet been read by mankind, for only great poets can read them.* Then I talked for a few minutes about the final exam, and then they got time to read.

After school, I had a writing conference with Isabella, who was trying to get her author project research done because she and her family were going to Peru for break. Isabella had said a day or so ago that she thought Thoreau's plain spoken or rustic diction was kind of a put-on, kind of hypocritical. He was, after all, a guy who could translate Latin and Greek, went to Harvard and so on. That triggered a conversation about George W. Bush and his use of "nuculer"—and I had assured the students that Bush altered his diction, inflection, accent and so forth to fit the occasion. He was a very smart guy. But that manipulation was not the same as Thoreau's. I didn't sense any hypocrisy in the tone, but I wanted to ask Isabella more about what she thought. Instead, we talked about what was going on in her creative nonfiction essay on Rothko, Melville, and Poe—it was probably twenty pages, fifteen over the limit. We talked about the school literary magazine, how no one read it, and how Emerson, Thoreau and friends published *The Dial*, pretty much for a small group of writers and like-minded thinkers. I handed Isabella a copy of *Granta*, and I told her maybe she could take it to Peru, and if it survived, she could return it. I opened up a page and there was a picture of Mark Twain sitting outside. Twain smokes a cigar and holds a kitten on his lap. Twain wears white.

A teacher's job is to artfully get out of the student's way. Then the student can be free to think and write—she can create something out of her new understanding. And maybe people will say you are a very good teacher, but you will know you had very little to do with it. It is how you step aside. It is the way that you allow the student to no longer fear retribution, to feel safe, to feel like she has space, finally, to do what she wants to do just for the sake of doing something well. A teacher's job is to not be a teacher at all. A little intelligent conversation. A sense of humor. A vision beyond the assessments of the school, state, country. Sure, why not? The day a student enters a school and finds no teachers and no SMART Boards, that is the day her education can begin. I've been in the process of disappearing for years—I see myself, a forty-six-year-old man, bearded: he wears a sweater with geometric patterns in muted colors—red wine, purples, black. He holds a yellow piece of chalk, chalk-dust on his wingtips. Then he's gone, and the piece of chalk floats for a second or two in space. It drops and hits the floor with a tap.

I wrote the words above in the morning and never had time to write my journal reactions to pages 101–120. I started each class with the same quotation: *I never found the companion that was so companionable as solitude.* Both classes recognized the figures of speech, especially paradox.

"Isn't paradox," asked Adrienne, "just irony because an opposite meaning is intended?"

Adrienne was well known among her peers for being slightly to very far off the meaning of what we discussed. But maybe she was inadvertently onto something here—and when Muhammad in the back row asked a similar question about oxymoron, we got into a few minutes about figures of speech and the opposite and/or disparate connections that are made in language. I tried to stop it by saying, "OK, OK, this is turning into a class on rhetoric and we have to get back to the pond."

"But why," asked another student, "do people always use *jumbo shrimp* as their example for oxymoron?"

So I reeled off my oxymoron list with explanations: *sweet sorrow, military intelligence* (Isabella said, with ironic tone, that she was "personally offended by that one"), and one that I claimed was near and dear to me: *psychiatric rehabilitation.* The class groaned. The list ended with *happy marriage*, and Dylan said, "Oh, that's terrible!" He had a big, deep voice, and I knew his parents just last year had gone through a divorce.

"Kidding, kidding," I added.

Isabella said, "You already said that one at the beginning of the year." I walked over to her desk, and in a mock aside, told her that it was difficult to teach when a student actually listened, and worse, remembered what I'd said, and I'd like her to not pay attention, *please*, to anything I said.

"You've asked me that before."

"And your point is?"

This satisfied her for the moment. Isabella would hold me accountable for every syllable.

After we circled up to talk about *Walden*, I told them that of course they could just go to SparkNotes.com. That was fine, but within a few seconds, I knew they could use their own brains and come up with understandings that were deeper and more nuanced and more interesting than the half-baked scholarship of half-baked scholars on-line. I also told them I owned stock in SparkNotes. So thank you.

"But how will you know that what we say is as good as SparkNotes.com?"

"I just read them. I mean, how am I supposed to come up with my own ideas to teach *Walden* anyhow? I'm just a country teacher."

I don't know when it started, but over the years, I have developed a catalogue of stock phrases: *I'm just a country teacher. I blame society. Can you be less specific? That's what scares me.*

"Mr. Miller, you blame society for everything."

"Somebody has to take the blame."

"Mr. Miller, you have the sense of humor of an eighth grader."

"Eighth grader? Really? Only eighth grade? Again, I blame society."

"Mr. Miller, I think I'm beginning to understand Transcendentalism."

"That's what scares me."

"Mr. Miller, you know that thing we're supposed to do when we quote an author?"

"Can you be any less specific?"

"Mr. Miller, where do you get your sweaters?" That's another element of being a teacher—students remembered your clothes more than anything else, except the Isabellas who quoted you back verbatim with a sardonic smile.

"Mr. Miller, I can talk about the Renaissance if you like." The meaning of the word *renaissance* had somehow come up in class, but I had said no—I knew Isabella could talk about the Renaissance for twenty minutes without a breath, and we were trying to understand American Literature. Before we had gotten to the daily quotation, Isabella and Kate had taken turns rattling off all the Roman Emperors from memory—it was showing off, an intellectual blood sport among their peers. Later that day, Kate would help run the Jane Austen Club where they'd exchange candy canes with Austenisms attached. In these moments and others, I felt the profound disconnect from what was taking place a few miles east in the city schools—an environment similar to the one I had taught in many years ago.

At the end of class, a couple of students hung around to check on papers and conferences. I continued the class discussion:

"Can a poet of molecules work in his garret to kill off, say, cancer, when he has to keep those grants rolling in?" That question had gotten Jake interested after he had bemoaned the loss of any time to contemplate, like he used to have in elementary school when he would read *Lord of the Rings* and then just go into a trance and think—he'd brought that example up to refute Adrienne's claim that what makes us happy is that we can go faster and that we have the internet and technology to make our lives better.

"Is that why sales of Prozac continue to rise?"

Adrienne's face turned to consternation.

Natalie said that once she had to spend forty-eight hours alone in the woods in Colorado. All she had was her *Harry Potter*—that was good for about six hours, and then she was on her own. She says she did not feel alone. She wrote a journal in the woods and most of the entries were about food.

We are the subjects of an experiment which is not a little interesting to me.

Well, I fell behind in my reading, so I had to play catch-up. I could barely remember what happened in school that day. It was Friday night, near midnight, and K was waiting tables at the local jazz club. Alfred Brendel played Bach through desktop speakers. Pre-divorce, back when I had left teaching and my family had lived for a year at the Institute for Advanced Study where my now ex-wife had been a visiting scholar—I became obsessed with Brendel's playing of Beethoven's *Bagatelles*. One day, I went for a walk in the institute's snowy woods, and during that walk, I could hear Beethoven's music in the sunshine as it rolled across the barren whiteness and stripped trees. I was learning about my isolation by taking steps in unmarked snow with Beethoven's musical annotations—I just could not put words to it. Snow was obliteration for some writers—I would say as much to a class when I finally returned to teaching.

It had been bizarre, for me, to be back in that part of the world—the place where I had met my ex-wife as an undergraduate, where we'd returned twenty years later with three sons in tow. In marriage therapy, she said it was when we were back east, when we had returned to the place where the relationship had started, that she realized her feelings had changed. Like a traditional piece of Western music, we had returned to the home key so the piece could end. I just didn't know. It had been my first year away from teaching, a year devoted to writing. I'd walked around the institute's woods and realized I enjoyed having time to read, think, and write. Two years later, my marriage was over. I had to change my life.

When K finally got home, we got into bed and the conversation turned philosophical.

At one point, K said I thought I deserved to be enlightened.

"I'm offended by that."

We argued about duality and how to move to oneness—which I insisted, un-Buddhistically, was the goal of Buddhist training.

"Do you know," K said, "how much *discipline* that takes?"

I protested.

"You and your fifty books on Buddhism," she said with humor and exasperation.

I curled up against K. She was passing out from exhaustion.

"It's OK if you stroke my hair," she whispered. I felt the coarse-softness of her hair between my fingers. I stroked her hair until her breathing calmed.

In the twenty-page section I had read before bed, I got to visit Thoreau in his bean-field. For the students, I'd compiled thirteen journal entry prompts, one of which was for the students to Tweet Thoreau—one student, Simon, would note the irony of such a prompt. For his seventh journal entry, another of my students will Tweet: *Going back to woods; visitors welcome, objects of charity not so. Will return to sell beans next year, though I have grown much more than beans here.*

Towards the end of his reading, I collected a few beans of my own: *Every man has to learn the points of the compass as often as he awakes, whether from sleep or any abstraction. Not till we are lost, in other words not till we have lost the world, do we begin to find ourselves, and realize where we are and the infinite extent of our relations.*

After divorce, it may seem that not only is the compass lost, but also the magnetic poles themselves play tricks. One night, post-divorce, after I'd moved into my new home in University City, I was awakened by the house shaking. During the first weeks of living alone, my heart knocked me around in bed before sleep, but this was different, and as I tried to sit up, I saw my dog, Bella, sliding sideways on the wood floor. *Fine, so this is it*, I thought, *let the ceiling crash down, whatever*—and then I just let my body relax and I fell into a deep sleep. Because of the divorce, I thought I'd lost the world—fatalism flooded in. But it was all an abstraction, asleep, a nightmare of an earthquake that really did shake the Midwest. Not that I had completely mastered this lesson by any means, nor did I think I deserved anything at all, but I did find myself in the fields or at the cobblers or looking into the workings of the village, and in those moments, I did know north from south, east from west, and found myself baiting nothingness to explore the infinite and star-filled good night.

Many a forenoon have I stolen away, preferring to spend thus the most valued part of the day; for I was rich, if not in money, in sunny hours and summer days, and spent them lavishly; nor do I regret that I did not waste more of them in the workshop or the teacher's desk.

I had to write a final exam review guide, a final exam—forty more pages of *Walden* to go—and back-grading stuffed deep into my teacher's desk not even touched.

Early on in the section titled "Baker Farm," Thoreau writes about standing in the very abutments of a rainbow's arch. It dazzles him, and it is as if he looks through colored crystal, a lake of rainbow light, *in which*, he writes, *I lived like a dolphin.* As I read those words, I thought, *aha!* I had had no idea why I'd been inspired to do my impersonation of a dolphin for my students—had I swum forwards in time at light speed to the moment in Thoreau that I was destined to read on a frigid, December night, after Thai food and not enough sake?

K was warm and asleep in the bed in the next room, and I read *Walden* until midnight. Did my late night thoughts get their *talaria*? It was more like I grew a dorsal fin.

When I got into bed, finally, K said it was too hot and that she had had bad dreams. *Where,* I wondered, *are Thoreau's bad dreams, and whom, may I ask, does he comfort, other than his own thinking? When I go a-fishing in his book, what pouts do I take from glaucous water? Maybe I'm just looking for my biological father, who spent twenty years hidden away in the Olympic Peninsula as a caretaker for a house on an island in Puget Sound—he outdid Thoreau by many years. I have a touch of that inside myself, methinks.*

Silence unspooled over years, and maybe that was the most accurate thing I could say. As a boy, I watched it ripple, and I did plenty of my own fishing: rainbow trout, sunfish, small-mouth bass, and I pulled, once, a black eel out of the Saugatuck River that whipped in the air as though it would crackle with lightning and thunder.

Then silence spread in circles. Still, I cast and continued to cast.

School was cancelled because of an ice storm, and that tied in nicely with the last class I taught, the day before, where I drew a "flow chart" that showed how Thoreau used nature as a lens to explore, to meditate, to analyze, to ponder, to consider: ethics, the self, spirituality, progress, society, and so on. Vaguely, I remembered talking about the pickerel of Walden and another passage where one can find the depth of a person's character: *if he is surrounded by mountainous circumstances, an Achillean shore, whose peaks overshadow and are reflected in his bosom, they suggest a corresponding depth in him.* At several points in class, intelligent ideas were shared about the book, and on the day that was iced out, they were supposed to review for the final exam.

Towards the end of *Walden*, I kept passing out as I read—maybe I was getting sick or maybe it was just the animal exhaustion of teaching. I had shaved off most of my beard. Thoreau left teaching because he would not administer corporal punishment—at least that's what the bio said. I left teaching to live in the woods that each writer must enter, and when I returned to the classroom, my life had changed. I had completed my second twenty-year circle only to start the third. It pushed out, like each word, from a new center, formed from that unknown alphabet, another twenty pages from within twenty pages, until, I figured, my life would merge with an unknown shore.

What is this stream of time? As I tried to finish *Walden*, my eyes crossed, so I left my desk to go lie down, to get under the heavy orange Korean blanket with two symmetrical tigers, growling, perched on clouds above flowers, to pass out. Downstairs, a child yelled, "Dinner!" Slowly, I pivoted onto my feet. I was disoriented. K had made chicken soup, and it scalded at first, but I blew on each spoonful and ate until I had gathered enough strength to regain a semblance of focus and balance. In my right ear, the sound of a washing machine: tinnitus. I wanted K in bed, to pull her close, to go off into dark sleep, and I hoped it would be as clear and deep as that pond in Concord, whose depth, like our character, can be measured. Outside our bedroom window, early in the mornings of late, we'd heard a rhythmic hooting, and maybe I would hear it tomorrow. Then, like so many other days, I'd get myself to school.

Adam Patric Miller's *A Greater Monster* was selected by Phillip Lopate as the winner of the 2013 Autumn House Press Nonfiction Prize. Miller has also won a Pushcart Prize and received a Notable Essay Selection in *The Best American Essays* series. His essays have been published in *Agni Magazine, The Florida Review*, and *Blue Earth Review*. During his years of teaching in an inner-city high school in Connecticut, Miller was twice voted Teacher of the Year. For his outstanding contributions to classroom teaching and for improving the quality of secondary education in Ohio, Miller was named a Jennings Scholar. As an undergraduate at Princeton University, Miller took a two-year leave to play the violin professionally. A highlight of those years was the chance to perform in Carnegie Hall. Miller lives with his wife and their blended family in St. Louis, Missouri.

THE AUTUMN HOUSE NONFICTION SERIES

Michael Simms, General Editor

Amazing Yoga: A Practical Guide to Strength, Wellness and Spirit
by Sean and Karen Conley

The Archipelago by Robert Isenberg

Between Song and Story: Essays for the Twenty-First Century
edited by Sheryl St. Germain and Margaret L. Whitford

Love for Sale and Other Essays by Clifford Thompson ■ 2012

Bear Season by Katherine Ayres

A Greater Monster by Adam Patric Miller ■ 2013

■ Winner of the Autumn House Nonfiction Prize

DESIGN AND PRODUCTION

Text and cover design by Kathy Boykowycz

Text set in Lucida Bright, designed in 1987 by Kris Holmes
Headings set in Frutiger, designed in 1975 by Adrian Frutiger

Printed by McNaughton and Gunn on Glatfelter Natural Offset,
an FSC certified paper